Drift and Badger and the Search for Uncle Mo

By
David Carter

TrackerDog Media

Drift & Badger

Drift and Badger and the Search for Uncle Mo
ISBN: 978-095597741-1
© Copyright David Carter 2009 © TrackerDog Media

First Edition
The right of David Carter to be identified as the Author of this Work has been asserted by him in accordance with the Copyright, Designs and Patents Act of 1988.

All rights reserved. No part of this book may be reproduced in any form or by any electronic or mechanical means, including information storage and retrieval systems, (with the exception of those purchasing by download), without permission in writing from the publishers, except by reviewers who may quote brief passages in reviews

Published by TrackerDog Media, 118 Ringwood Road, Walkford, Christchurch, Dorset, England BH23 5RF Email: supalife@aol.com
Wholesale enquiries welcomed
Enquiries also welcomed from overseas and secondary publishers

Please visit the websites:

www.driftandbadger.com
www.trackerdogmedia.co.uk
www.davidcarter.eu

for more information on this and other books, articles and projects

Drift and Badger and the Search for Uncle Mo

This one is for
**Anne
who
really likes
this story**

Drift and Badger and the Search for Uncle Mo

One

The forest in autumn is one of God's great sights when the leaves turn colour and bask in that special golden light. The forest is home to many magical creatures and toward the end of the year it provides the greatest spectacle on earth. Nothing compares, nor ever will.

And so it was when Drift was born, unseasonably late, dropping from his mother on to the mossy bank she had so carefully chosen for his birth. Drift would be the last fawn of the year and would always struggle against his bigger, brasher, brethren.

That didn't concern his mother, nor Drift himself; for he had yet to meet any of his kinfolk for she had trekked deep within the forest, well away from the frantic herds, especially to give birth.

Within minutes he was on his feet, shaking and shivering in the October wind as his mother washed and licked him clean, just in time for a good feed. The first feed is always the most precious when the milk is at its richest and after that, within an hour, he was ready to follow her anywhere.

There was so much to see in the forest and a great deal to learn with little time to lose. Drift followed her from the edge of the woods to the meadow and watched her as she paused and nodded ahead.

'Look,' she said, 'the trees are turning colour, reds and yellows, amber and gold, they are normally green, you see, it will be winter before long and you are so small. We will have to fatten you up as fast as we can, or you won't see the spring.'

'Yes, mother.'

Far away a dog barked. Drift stood petrified, his mother confidently standing upright beside him.

'It is all right, little one,' she said. 'It is only a dog. Their bark is far worse than their bite. All noise and no dignity. They have lost their independence. They have sold their souls and gone to live with the humanthings.'

'What is a humanthing?'

'Two legged creatures. Nasty beasts to be avoided at all costs. They stare at you and I can see what they are thinking.'

'And what are they thinking, mother?'

'How they can…how they can…' his mother hesitated, not wishing to unduly frighten her new fawn. There would be plenty of time to teach the youngster of the terrible ways of the humanthings. 'How they can tease you, that's all,' she finished off. 'How they can tease you.'

They came to a road, straight and true, for roads criss-crossed the forest everywhere.

Drift watched his mother glance one way, then the other, then back the first way, and dash across.

'Come along,' she shouted. 'Don't dilly-dally! Don't shilly-shally!'

The youngster trotted after her and re-joined his mother.

'These are roads,' she explained, 'they are *very* dangerous places.'

Dangerous, thought Drift, he couldn't see how they could possibly be dangerous.

'Cars and trucks roar up and down at all hours of the day and night, and they don't stop.'

'What is a car, and what is a truck?'

And as if to answer Drift's question a large black car noisily approached from the left.

'Hurry,' she said, 'into the trees,' and she darted for cover. Drift followed mighty quick, anxious not to remain alone in the open.

In the safety of the woods they turned about and watched the car flash by; smoke belching from the rear end. Inside sat a single humanthing, a young male with a wolfish grin set on its hideous face.

'That's a car,' said mother, 'with a humanthing inside,' her nose turned up in disgust, 'and they rarely stop, I told you. Trucks are even worse. They are bigger and harder and even more horrid. You mark my words, young fellow, you must never dally on the roads, never, for if you do, you…'

She didn't have to say anymore. Drift instinctively knew that roads and cars and trucks, and most especially, humanthings, spelt terrible danger.

'Come,' she said, 'we have a long way to go to reach the herds. I can't wait for you to meet uncle Mo and all the rest. He will be so pleased to see you for you are so like your father, you are, and that's a fact.'

'Where is father?' asked Drift.

'He's gone now,' she said in a hurry and in the way she said it, Drift knew better than to ask any more.

An hour later it began to grow dark.

'What is happening, mamma?' said a panicked Drift, glancing at the blackening sky.

'The sun is going down, that's all. It will soon be totally dark, and there is no moon tonight.'

'I don't like it, mamma, and what's a moon?'

'There is nothing to be frightened of young Drift, and the moon will come back soon. It is like the sun but cold and not so bright and only glows when the sun is resting. Tonight it will grow cold and there will be sounds aplenty from the noisy creatures that live that way. I am sorry to say they have never learnt any manners. They cannot remain quiet like the rest of us, no consideration, my mother used to say, but we have to forgive them for they live in the forest just as we do. They know no better, and they will never change. Stay close to me, and never be frightened of the dark. In time you will come to realise it is your friend, the darkness is a good time. You will learn to enjoy the night and you will always be safer in the darkness than during the hours of daylight. The night is your best friend. Humanthings are afraid of the dark, but we are not… never.'

'I see,' said Drift, still unconvinced, for he liked the colours of the forest, as the sun slipped slowly down below the trees and fell out of sight. The temperature dropped rapidly as they travelled across the countryside and a little later, close by, a fox barked.

'Err!' said Drift. 'What is that?'

His mother stopped in her tracks, her nose and ears twitching.

'It's a fox,' she whispered dismissively. 'Nothing to worry about. They are all mouth and no brains. If the darn thing comes close to you give it a good kick in the chops. That will send it on its way. Big teeth, tiny minds, my old mother always used to say about foxes, and she was right at that as well. Foxes are clueless idiots. They think they own the forest but they do not. I have never seen a fox face up to a stag yet. Never. They haven't got a clue. Masters of the forest, they couldn't master an earwig.'

Drift grinned and thought better than to ask what an earwig was.

Away to the right, in the dark undergrowth, they could both now see the fox moving away, deeper into the thicket, its brush of a tail swaying gently this way and that as it disappeared into the brambles.

'I am hungry, mamma.'

'You will always be hungry. It is natural at your age. But we can't stop yet awhile. We need to cross the river. After that, we can stop and you can feed to your heart's content. It isn't far now.'

The river was twenty feet across but it hadn't rained for a week and the water level was low and it was nothing more than a gentle trot across. Drift enjoyed the first sensation of the cold river on his legs and feet, kicking up the water in fun, splashing his mother, giggling.

'Don't do that, son. You must learn to travel through the forest in silence. It is rule number one. Never attract undue attention to yourself. You just never know who is out there, who may be listening. Travel stealthily. Know where others are, but keep your presence a secret.'

'Sorry, mamma. I will try.'

'Think nothing of it, but learn your lessons well, Drift. Take a quick drink now while you have the chance and then we shall be on our way.'

How clever his mother was, he thought, how wise and wonderful.

The water was cold and sweet and he filled his belly, though he made sure to leave just a little room for the warm milk he knew would soon be coming his way.

An hour later they came to a large clearing. Through the middle of the open forest ran another road, wider and grimmer and more treacherous than the first.

'This is one of the busiest roads through the entire forest,' she said. 'Always treat it with the utmost of respect. There is great danger here.'

The tone in her voice alerted Drift. It worried him that there could be anything so dangerous, so terrible, that even his impressive mother might be afraid of it.

They tiptoed toward the highway, his mother peering through the darkness one way and then the other. Her ears twitched, her nose too. Not a sound, other than a distant owl that was showing off to its mate. Hoot! Hoot!

'Shut-up!' she whispered, and then she lowered her head and listened to the ground, for occasionally she could tell if danger approached from distant vibrations. Nothing. Silence. It all looked good. A favourable moment to cross. In front of the road was a small fence with another similar barrier on the far side. In the darkness they couldn't see it from where they were, but she knew it was there all right.

'There's a small fence,' she whispered, 'on both sides. I'll show you where it is. You have to jump the fence, cross the road, jump the far fence, and make for the cover of the trees where I shall be waiting. Understand?'

'Yes mamma,' replied Drift sidling up to her warm body, close enough for her to feel his shivers. 'There is nothing to worry or be afraid about. Just do as I say and be quick about it.'

'I will, mamma. I understand.'

'Good, now here it is, look, the first fence.'

To her it was nothing and she could hop over it with little effort as if it didn't exist, but to Drift it was a sizeable obstacle, large logs running from left to right supported by stakes driven into the ground every twelve feet or so.

'I'm going over,' she said. 'Take great care. I'll see you on the other side in trees.'

'Yes mamma,' he said, forcing himself not to cry.

Then she was away, hopping over the fence, cantering across the road, disappearing into the darkness. He heard her hooves clopping on the tarmac, he heard her leap the far fence and then slowly the noise of her running decreased until there was only silence.

For the first time in his young life Drift was alone and he didn't care for it. He didn't like it at all. He glanced about him. Nothing at all, only the sound of the old owl. He wanted to be with his mother again and the only way to achieve that was to dash across the highway. He feebly hopped at the fence, hitting it, hurting his face, falling backward, banging and grazing his knees.

'Ow!' he muttered, struggling to stand upright.

'Come along!' he heard her calling from the far side.

With all his might he leapt at the fence again, clearing it with inches to spare. He ran to the road, setting his front hoof on the hard blacktop as if to check the foreign substance. He glanced one way and then the other. Nothing. He ambled on to the road, pausing a moment to feel the strange smooth surface beneath his feet. It had a peculiar smell. Not unlikeable, but quite different to anything he had ever smelt before. In the next moment he felt as if he were standing on the surface of the sun. He was bathed in the brightest light he had ever known. Terrible sounds came from the left as if from the gates of hell itself.

Beeeeep! Beeeeep! Beeeeep!

Drift froze. He turned and stared toward the pair of blazing white suns that were rushing down on him, angry white eyes that seemed to stare right through him, casting hideous shadows beyond him into the night that frightened him to his soul. The crashing noise of the truck's engine and dashing wheels became unbearable. Time seemed to stand still.

Beeeeep! Beeeeep! Beeeeeeeeeeeeeep!!!

Drift tried in vain to move but was stricken with fear. His day old limbs simply would not obey.

The gobbling lights were almost upon him when in a whir of movement and energy his mother dashed from the trees, on to the road, and butted him across the highway and backward clean over the first fence.

Beeeeep! Beeeeep! Beeeeeeeeeeeeeep!!! Continued the truck as it flashed by, delivering a fearsome blow to his mother's shoulder as it did so.

Thankfully Drift didn't see it, though he heard the loud bump well enough as the lorry collided with the mother. He righted himself in time to see the truck from hell speeding away without ever slowing, up and over a small hill and out of sight to the right. He frantically shook himself and whimpered and leapt the fence back on to the road.

'Mamma!' he cried. 'Mamma, where are you?'

Silence, but for the distant sound of the truck moving away on the far side of the hill. Even the funny fool of an owl had fallen silent.

Drift leapt the second fence and frantically ran around the grass.

'Mamma,' repeated Drift, as he sniffed for her warm body.

A moment later he found her, twenty yards clear of the tarmac, lying on her side as if asleep.

'Mamma,' yelled Drift. 'I am so sorry, mamma. Are you all right, mamma? Please say you are all right.'

But mamma remained silent, and from that day onward, always would.

Two

For three days and nights Drift wandered the forest alone, drinking from the brooks and streams, but never eating. He began to lose what little weight he possessed. He began to lose heart. The moon returned and lit up the night sky as Drift cowered in the undergrowth.

On the fourth night he ventured out, desperate for food. He crept into a clearing wondering where his uncle Mo might be when he heard a sound he had never heard before. It was a long yawn, followed by someone or something, licking their lips.

Drift stood bolt still. He was terrified. In the moonlight he saw a creature amble into the clearing. It stopped before him and casually said: 'Oh, hello.'

Drift nodded a greeting.

'Never seen you around these parts before,' said the stranger.

'I have never been round these parts before. I hope you don't mind me asking, but what are you, exactly?'

'Me?' said the stranger, standing up on his back legs and glancing at his paws. 'I'm a badger, don't you know. Can't you tell? I thought everyone could identify a blinking badger.'

'All badgers are bad!' uttered Drift without thinking, though he regretted saying it as soon as the words flew from his lips.

'Eh? Sorry you feel that way, young fella. Why do you say that anyhow?'

'It's obvious isn't it? It's in your name. Bad-gers. You are a Badger. Stands to reason. You must be bad!'

'Don't talk such tommyrot! There is good and bad in every family. I know some of your lot who are rotten to the core. Good and bad in all, that's what I say.'

'I'm sorry,' said Drift, feeling guilty. 'I didn't mean you personally.'

'Should jolly well think not,' said the badger, rubbing sleep from his black eyes.

'What is your name?' asked Drift.

'Just Mister Badger will do.'

'You must have a proper name.'

The badger looked about as if to check they weren't being watched or listened to.

'I do as it happens, but I am not so keen on it.'

'Go on, do tell, I won't tell anyone else.'

'Promise?'

Drift nodded his head.

'And you won't laugh?'

'Course not.'

'Well it's Daisy if you must know.'

Drift stifled a laugh.

'See! I knew you would laugh!'

'I am sorry, er…Daisy, but isn't that a girl's name?'

'Not in our family it isn't. Daisy Willowpop if you must know. Pleased to meet you,' said the badger and he reached forward and patted Drift on the snout. 'And you are?'

'My name is Drift.'

'Drift what?'

'Just Drift.'

'You're a red deer, aren't you?'

'Am I?'

'Yep, should think so, by the look of you, with that coat of yours. Methinks you'll be a big strong stag one day, you know that, don't you?'

'That's what my mother always said. She said I'd be the king of stags with a royal set of antlers, something to be proud of, one day far in the future.'

'It's possible, in time, though I never did quite understand all that tree growing out of the head caper. Wouldn't like it meself. Must be most uncomfortable.'

'I really can't say, I don't know,' said the fawn.

'Where is your mother anyway?'

'Er…well…she's gone away.'

'Eh. Oh well, it happens that way sometimes. Chin up kid; you'll be all right. Most folks round this part of the forest are decent enough. Just keep off the roads and keep away from the humanthings.'

'I will, Daisy, for sure, I will.'

'Well nice to meet you, Drift, but I can't stand around here all night gossiping. I have just woken up and I am as hungry as a fox in a hen coop.'

'I am hungry too,' said Drift. 'Starving to be exact.'

'Well, there is some good grazing down there in the clearing. Help yourself, young fella, I don't want it. I am off in search of juicy worms.'

'I can't,' said Drift, 'I am not yet ready to eat grass.'

'Oh I see,' said the badger, thinking hard. 'You must be starving hungry,' and Daisy stood back and looked more carefully at the fawn and the bones he could see clearly under his tousled coat, and realised he was exactly right. His ribs were showing and that wasn't a good sign. Daisy lifted his paw to his head and glanced up at the moon and said, 'I just might be able to help you there, boy.'

'Eh? How?'

'There's a fat badger back at the sett called Grelda. She lost her kit in the big storm. She could give you a good feed I should think, if I spoke to her nicely.'

'Oh would you, Daisy? Would you do that? That would be so lovely.'

'Come on then, follow me, and we'll find out.'

They crossed the clearing, darted through a stand of silver birch trees that were losing their leaves, and came to a gurgling brook. Daisy skipped across a fallen tree while Drift danced straight through the burbling water. Ahead of them now was a large mound covered in neatly trimmed grass. To the right of the mound was a big black hole.

'Best if you wait here a mo,' said Daisy. 'I'll go on down and see how the land lies. Won't be a tick,' and with that his black and white behind disappeared down the hole.

A moment later Drift thought he heard voices. He leant toward the hole and listened. He was right, he could hear voices.

'Oh no, Daisy,' someone was saying, 'I am not washed and clean. You could have given me more warning.'

'But he is such a nice little fella, Drift's his name, and so hungry, you'll love him to bits.'

'No, I really can't be doing with it. No means no.'

'What would you say if I promised to bring you back a fine supper?'

'Really, do you mean it? A really fine supper, mind.'

'I am a badger of my word. I do's what I says.'

'Oh all right then, but please tell him I haven't had time to tidy up. The place is a pigsty.'

The next moment Daisy popped up from the hole, grinning triumphantly.

'She'll do it. She'll jolly well do it. What did I tell you?'

'I know,' said Drift, 'I heard.'

'Go on then, get yourself down there and feast before she changes her mind.'

Drift nodded his head and then remembered to say thank you as his mother always said he should, and stuck his head into the hole.

From the outside the hole looked huge, but for all his tinyness Drift had broad shoulders and he simply could not squeeze in. Worse than that he was now stuck fast.

'I'm stuck!' he shouted, 'I am jolly well stuck!'

'Oh crikey,' said Daisy, and he reached down and grabbed the fawn's back legs and roughly dragged him from the hole.

In the moonlight Drift staggered to his feet, shaking his head vigorously, for he knew there must be mud all over his snout and neck.

'You look a bit dirty now,' said Daisy. 'Bit of a mess.'

'And whose fault is that?'

'Here,' said Daisy, and he reached across and wiped the mud from Drift's face with his paw. 'You can't be visiting Grelda with a face like that. Frighten her you would. Frighten her to death.'

'What do we do now?'

The badger smiled and waggled his claws in front of Drift's eyes.

'All is not yet lost, young Drift, my friend. Come on, there is a back way in. We badgers are not all stupid, you know.'

'I hope it's bigger than the front,' muttered Drift, but Daisy didn't hear that for he had scurried round to the back of the mound. Drift followed keenly, growing hungrier by the minute. The badger was right, for there was a larger, squarer hole that appeared to lead down to the centre of the mound.

Drift glanced at the entrance and back at Daisy.

'Are you sure it will be all right?'

'Course I am. I fixed it. Said so didn't I. You get down there right sharpish.'

Drift shook his head one last time and threw himself into the hole, half expecting to become stuck fast as he had before, but this time he didn't. Instead he found himself in a small tunnel and from there he could see light before him flickering at the far end. He pressed on and suddenly the tunnel opened out into a large and cosy room.

To the left was a chunky three-draw chest of drawers. Someone had painted the drawers red, green and blue and on the top of the chest sat a stubby candle that threw its flickering light across the sett. On the other side of the room was a large ancient rocking chair that had belonged to the badgers for longer than anyone could remember, and in the chair, half sitting, half lying on her back was an old, and it has to be said, very fat, badger.

'Hello,' she said, 'and you must be the one they call Drift.'

'Yes, I am, thank you for seeing me, Grelda.'

'My name is Grelda 'tis true, but you must call me Mrs Whizz.'

'Yes Mrs Whizz, whatever you say.'

'And you are hungry are you?'

'Starving.'

'Mmm. Well I may be able to help you there, but a deal's a deal. Daisy promised me faithfully he would bring me a super supper. One good turn deserves another you know.'

'I am sure he will, Mrs Whizz.'

'You just make sure that he does, young Drift, or one feed will be all you get.'

'I will Mrs Whizz. I will, for sure.'

'Mmm, well you seem a nice enough little deer, I am willing to give you a chance,' and the old badger shifted in her chair as if making ready. 'Well, what you waiting for? Get on with it before I change my mind.'

'Yes,' said Drift uncertainly, approaching the badger. 'I have never tasted badger milk before.'

'Then you have a rare treat in store for yourself. Delicious it is. Milk's milk aint it?'

'Yes,' said Drift, his mouth as dry as dead wood at just the mention of the words delicious and milk.

'Well go on then, get on with it, get started.'

Afterwards, outside in the moonlight, Drift felt as if he could run to the end of the earth and back. He'd fed until bursting and now he was looking for Daisy with Mrs Whizz's parting words lingering in his ears.

'Find that Daisy, and make sure he lives up to his part of the bargain!'

Right on cue Daisy ambled from the undergrowth and he was carrying something strange.

'Oh, there you are,' said Drift. 'I have been looking for you.'

'Fed well, have you?'

'I have,' grinned Drift.

'Good was it?'

'Exquisite, I can't tell you how good it was.'

'I knew Grelda would see you all right. She's a decent enough old critter.'

'Have you anything for her?' asked Drift. 'She's hungry too.'

'I do as it happens, here in this box.'

'What is it?'

'It's a hamburger.'

'A what?'

'A hamburger. Yep, delicious it is, with fried onions. If it wasn't for my promise I'd have scoffed it myself long before now.'

'Show me,' said Drift.

Daisy came closer and carefully opened the yellow plastic box.

Drift lowered his nose inside and breathed in.

'Yuck! I don't like the smell of that!'

'Well I don't suppose deer are interested in hamburgers.'

'What's it made of?'

'You really don't want to know, Drift.'

'Where did you get it?'

'Ah, now that's the funny thing. I was out feeding in the clearing near to the highway when one of those open topped cars came out of nowhere, music blaring, trying hard to impress the female I should think, all that kind of caper, when all of a sudden the male humanthing casually tossed this box high into the air and out of the car. It bounced once on the road and then rolled on to the grass. I had to be quick mind, because I knew the old owl was about and he certainly likes hamburgers. I grabbed the box before anyone else could get to it and scurried back into the woods, and here I am now.'

'Why is there a piece missing, there, look,' said Drift.

Daisy seemed a little guilty but said: 'Looks like the humanthing took one bite and didn't like it. They are all overfed, that lot. Fussy blighters they are, fussy eaters too, won't even eat earthworms, no wonder so few creatures will have anything to do with them. It's not a big problem, I'll just smooth that corner off a bit, Grelda's short sighted as it is, she'll never notice.'

'If you say so.'

'I do say. I am taking it down to her now, that should guarantee you another good feed tomorrow, and after that, I'll show you round this part of the forest if you like. I could show you what's what and who's who. That kind of thing.'

'Would you? Oh, that would be great, Daisy. I am going to call you a goodger from now on.'

Daisy giggled. 'A goodger indeed, whatever next. Won't be a mo, I'll be back in a tick.'

Three

The moon was high in the sky when they set off, skirting the woods to avoid the roads. They came to a large meadow where highland cattle were often to be seen but that night the field was deserted and quiet. Or was it? They both noticed movement in the meadow at the same moment.

'Quiet,' whispered Daisy, as they hunched down into the long grass.

'What is it?' asked Drift

'Can't tell yet, though I think it's Hexy.'

'Who the heck is Hexy?' whispered Drift, his attention taken for a moment by three pheasants squabbling over something in the low trees behind them.

'He's the resident fox round these parts,' said Daisy. 'Hexagon to give him his full name. Between you and me, he is a bit of a weed.'

In the moonlight they watched the creature leaping and pouncing on non-existent prey.

'Yep, it's Hexy all right, said the badger, 'I'd recognise that odd movement anywhere,' and Daisy stood on his back feet, placed his right front claw into his mouth, and let out a fearsome whistle that rocketed across the meadow and echoed back to them from the tall trees beyond.

The fox stood perfectly still, glaring toward the sound.

'Oi, Hexy!' bellowed the badger. 'Come over here, there's someone I want you to meet.'

In the next moment the fox was trotting on tiptoe toward where they were standing and in the next second they could see the fox growing bigger and bigger as it closed on them until he was standing right in front of them.

'Well, well, well,' said the fox through a silly voice that echoed down its nose, 'and what have we here?'

'This is a new pal of mine,' said Daisy, 'his name's Drift. Drift, meet Hexagon, our local and slightly crazy, but tough, fox.'

The fox smiled, flashing his rows of razor sharp teeth, revelling in his tough reputation, not for a moment realising that the badger was teasing.

'Pleased to meet you,' said Drift, still remembering his mother's advice about foxes. *Kick 'em in the chops!*

'Likewise I am sure,' said Hexagon, in his slightly effete voice. 'Good job old badger here told me you were one of his friends, or otherwise I would have had you for my dinner.'

'Take no notice of him,' said Daisy, 'the biggest dinner he is likely to find tonight is a dung beetle.'

Drift tittered. Badger laughed too at his own little joke.

'Ha, ha, I'm sure,' said the fox. 'It just goes to show, you don't know me that well.'

'Never mind all that now,' said Daisy, 'the thing is, Hex my old gingernut, Drift has lost his pals. You haven't seen a herd of deer round these parts by any chance, have you?'

'Bit careless to lose one's herd, what, don't you think?'

'Can you help or can't you?' said Daisy, trying hard to keep the annoyance from his lips.

The fox took a big step backward and focussed more clearly on the fawn.

'What is he? A red?'

Badger nodded. Drift did too.

'No reds round here for a while now, not so far as I know, may be four or five weeks. Think they all went north toward the Farley Enclosure, though I couldn't be sure.'

'That's a huge estate on the far side of the forest,' muttered Daisy. 'If the reds are as far away as that it could take ages to find them.'

'Sorry I can't be of any more assistance,' schmoozed the fox. 'You could try Langley. He might know. That is the best advice I can give to you, my old black and white chum. Sorry, must go now, out hunting you understand, on the trail of a significant meal, know what I mean?' and he tapped his snout with his front paw and winked and turned about and loped away across the meadow, his brush of a tail wafting this way and that like a cold draught in the sett.

'What a prune,' whispered Daisy.

'He didn't seem all that bad,' said Drift.

'He's not, but he *is* a prune, you have to admit,' and they both laughed aloud together.

'Come on,' said Daisy, 'I have an idea.'

They continued on their way along the side of the meadow, rarely venturing far from the trees.

'Who's Langley?' asked Drift.

'He's the head owl. He's all right is Langley, and there is not much that goes on in these parts that Langley doesn't know about. If your mob are in the district, Langley will surely know.'

'I do hope so,' said Drift.

'He's usually to be found on the Wondering Cross. Come on, we'll head down that way.'

They came to a gully where the trees fell sharply away. They heard water burbling and splashing below them and Drift instinctively knew there would be a cool drink to be had at the base of the ravine.

Sure enough there it was, but the rivulet was narrow and surprisingly deep and the water was flowing faster than any brook or river Drift had ever seen before.

'Take care crossing,' said Daisy, 'you wouldn't be the first to fall in and make a spectacle of themselves.'

At the narrowest point Drift leapt across, jumping harder than he'd ever jumped before and clearing the brook with feet to spare.

'Blimey, you're a good jumper, I'll give you that,' said Daisy, still looking for the narrowest point to scurry across, though he made it well enough, his stubby little tail dipping in the cold water at the last moment.

'Oooh!' said Daisy in complete surprise. 'That's freezing.'

They scampered up the far bank and through the trees, scuffling their feet in the carpets of golden leaves, and then came to a barely used lane that was made of rough gravel. A quick look left and right, nothing coming, no lights, no sound, and onward into a new field of year old Christmas trees, all planted in neat lines like soldiers on parade.

'What is this place?' asked Drift, looking about, sniffing the base of the nearest tree.

'Humanthings at work again,' said the badger, dismissively, shaking his head. 'Crackers they are. Every year they plant these trees and just when they are getting established, when the insects and spiders have moved in and hunkered down for the winter, toward the end of the year when the nights are longest and the days shortest, they come along with noisy and smelly machines and cut them all down again and cart them off to heaven knows where for heaven knows what. Crackers they are, I tell thee. Crackers!'

It did seem a little crazy to plant cute little trees and cut them down again before they had had a chance to grow, but for the moment there was another thing that had caught Drift's interest.

'What is the Wondering Cross?'

'Oh that!' said the badger, scampering over a fallen tree, stubbing his toe. 'Blast and dammit! You might well ask.'

'Humanthings again?' suggested Drift.

'Correctamundo, got it in one, my young friend. Long before my time it was, they came along with a huge mucky, smoky truck full of big grey stones with four of the foulest smelling humanthings the forest had ever been forced to endure. All day and half of the next they set about piling up those stones into a huge cross, and when they'd done, do you know what they did? They ran away and left it. Just like that. Ran away and left it! Now it sits all alone in the middle of the forest brooding. You can tell how unhappy it is just by looking at the poor thing. It's got no friends, no one to talk to, no point in being there so far as I can see, out in all weathers, being tinkled on and scratched and worse by every creature under the sun and stars, just standing there, its arms outstretched for all eternity. My goodness, it must get so terribly tired, and bored too, I shouldn't wonder.'

'But why?' asked Drift.

'That's what we would all like to know. Apparently after they had gone, word went round the forest like wildfire and everyone was summoned to a big meeting at the cross. The story goes that one of the carthorse's ancestors, a fellow called Jermaine, is supposed to have said: *I wonder what it is for.*'

'Now we all know that the horses are not the brightest figs on the tree, speak as I find mind, a horse had never harmed me or any of my lot, but apparently one of Langley's ancestors said in reply: From now on that's what we will call it: The Wondering Cross, and it has been called that ever since.'

'How peculiar,' said Drift.

'Ah, but it gets stranger yet,' said Daisy. 'Once a year they all come to the cross, the humanthings, I mean, and do you know what they do? They place bundles of red flowers all round it, sort of decorate it up kind of thing, as if it is some kind of Goddess.'

'But why?'

'Lord only knows, but the really sad thing about it is, the flowers are not even real!! They are fakes! Phonies! Useless to your lot, and the horses and cows, who would of course have scoffed the lot, given half the chance. The first year they were placed there one of the big fellows tried to eat the darn things and nearly choked to death.'

'Goodness,' said Drift. 'I really don't understand the humanthings at all.'

'No one does, Drift, no one does. That's another reason why they are treated with such suspicion. Eh up, here we are then, here it is, we have arrived at the Wondering Cross.'

They sauntered from the trees and gawped up at the frightening looking structure set deep within the forest. In the moonlight it looked dark and unforgiving, its arms outstretched as if it were about to strike down on any unsuspecting passer by.

'I don't like it at all,' stammered Drift. 'This isn't a nice place. It seems so cold.'

'It's all right,' said the badger. 'We all thought that at first, though it does have a menacing look about it, I agree, but it has been here for ten ages now and to my certain knowledge it has never harmed a living soul.'

'No red flowers today,' said Drift, busily sniffing around the base.

'Nope, though they are due again soon if my sense of timing is still working.'

'And you meet the owl here?'

'Yep, he's here most nights. He sits on the top cooing, or wooing, or ooing or whatever it is that owls do.'

Right on cue Langley came in to land. They could hear him long before they could see him, his wings beating furiously as he lost speed and height and slowly descended to the very top of the cross. The moment he had folded his wings away he let rip a blowing: Twit-twa-wooooo!!!

'What a racket,' whispered Drift.

'Quiet,' said Daisy, 'or we'll learn nothing.'

The badger stood upright and smiled up toward the top of the cross. The moon was directly behind the owl and it lit him up like silver.

'Good evening, Langley,' shouted Daisy, 'so pleased to make your acquaintance again.'

The owl glanced down, one eye examining each of the newcomers and then said, 'Well if it isn't my old friend, Daisy Willowpop, unless I am much mistaken.'

'He knows your real name,' tittered Drift.

'Yes all right, all right,' said Daisy, anxious to press on with matters in hand. 'Of course he does. Owls like to know everything, don't you know that?' And then he shouted up at the cross, 'that's me Langley, and I have brought my new pal along to see you. His name is Drift.'

'I can see that,' said Langley, both eyes now focused on the fawn, 'I have seen this young fellow before.'

'You have?'

The owl nodded.

'Where, when?' asked Daisy.

'Not a pleasant occasion, I have to say. Down by the highway. He was with his mother at the time.'

'Ah that,' said Daisy, 'it's best not to concentrate on that. Say no more.'

'For once you are right, Daisy Willowpop. Now what is it I can do for you? I can't stay for long gossiping all night; I have a date with a run of rats at the old barn. I mustn't be late or that impostor from Blue China Farm will be there before me.'

'The thing is,' said Daisy, 'we are looking for Drift's people.'

'The big red herd, you mean?'

'Yep, that's the one.'

'No point in looking round here then.'

'They've gone?'

'Weeks ago.'

'Do you know where they are now?'

'No, I don't, though there is a rumour they have travelled to the Farley Enclosure.'

'We've heard that too. Couldn't you possibly fly high and see if you can spot them?' persisted Daisy. 'I'll bet you can see for miles when you are up there in the sky.'

''Tis true, Daisy, we can see for miles, but the Farley Enclosure is a lot further than that, and another thing, those darned reds are mighty hard to spot if they don't wish to be seen. Masters of camouflage they are, you must know what they are like. They travel in darkness and often under the umbrella of the trees. Hard to spot they are, jolly hard. No, what you really need is an LTF.'

'What's an LTF?' said Drift and badger at precisely the same moment.

'Long Term Flyer,' said the owl. 'Don't you know anything about aeronautics? The swallows would have helped you of course, but they have all left now to chase the sun. No, the only one I can think of who might possibly help you is Bread n' Cheese.'

Daisy exhaled nosily and tapped his foot and shook his head.

'Oh no, not Bread n' Cheese.'

'Who's Bread n' Cheese?' asked Drift.

'He's as daft as a brush,' moaned Daisy, before continuing his conversation with the owl.

'He is a very difficult creature to do business with.'

'Yes, he is, I will give you that,' said Langley, 'but he is a long term flyer, which is what you need, and he would do a good job for you, just so long as you adequately rewarded him of course.'

'Who's Bread n' Cheese?' repeated Drift.

Daisy frowned and clicked his tongue. 'Where shall we find him?'

Langley turned his head right round and glanced up at the moon. 'Should be here in about an hour I should say.'

'Who is Bread n' Cheese?' said Drift again, kicking the ground.

'We'll wait here,' said Daisy, 'and thanks for your help, Langley.'

'Think nothing of it,' shouted the owl, and with that he stretched out his heavy wings, began beating, kicked off from the top of the cross, and flew across the face of the moon and away over the old big redwoods that have stood in that part of the forest for nigh on a thousand years.

Drift came and sat on the bottom step that surrounded the base of the cross and crossed his legs.

'Are you going to tell me who the heck Bread n' Cheese is or not, or do I have to talk to myself all night?'

'Cuckoo,' said Daisy.

'He's cuckoo?' asked Drift.

'No he isn't cuckoo, well he is really, he is a genuine cuckoo, it's just that he thinks he's a swallow, the poor confused boy, because he was raised by swallows you see, 'cept he doesn't go in for all that chasing the sun business every year. He's supposed to of course, but he's so confused he stays here with us, but when he's in the sky he likes to fly around like a swallow, covering long distances as if he were a swallow, though he is not as quick or as graceful. You follow?'

'Like an LTF?' beamed Drift.

Daisy smiled. 'Aye, that's right, you've got it, Drift. If anyone can find the big red herd, Bread n' Cheese is the bird.'

'And dare I ask why he is called *Bread n' Cheese?*'

Daisy giggled aloud. 'You'll see, just as soon as he gets here.'

Four

The silence of the forest was broken by a strange noise that came from the right cross beam of the Wondering Cross.

Breadandcheese! Breadandcheese! Breadandcheese!

'Eh up, he's arrived,' said Daisy, and they both peered upward.

'Why does he make that peculiar noise?' asked Drift.

'The best guess is,' started Daisy, 'that because he thinks he's a swallow, yet he's really a cuckoo, his call, that *Breadandcheese!* nonsense that you heard, is a cross between a Cuckoo! Cuckoo! and the twittering sound a swallow really makes. Kind of a hybrid call, sort of thing. That's what everyone thinks anyway, and that's why he's called what he is. The poor boy is obviously seriously confused.'

''Ello Mush,' said the creature perched on the arm of the cross in a strange high-pitched voice.

Daisy lifted his paw and cupped it round his mouth and whispered to Drift, 'and another thing, he can never remember anyone's name, which in my case is no bad thing, so he calls everyone Mush.'

Daisy glanced up.

'Hello Bread n' Cheese. We have been waiting here for you.'

'Have you, Mush. And why would that be?'

'We have a little job for you.'

'Oh yes, and what might that be?'

'We are in need of an LTF, a reconnaissance job, kind of thing.'

'I am an LTF,' he said proudly. 'I am an LTF. I am a swallow, don't you know.'

'Yes, of course you are, Bread n' Cheese, that's exactly why we came here to see you.'

Drift watched the fat bird's chest swell with pride.

'Quite so, Mush, quite so. So what is it you want exactly?'

'My friend Drift here has lost his herd.'

'Oh yes, red is he?'

Daisy nodded and continued. 'We want you to find them if you can, fly off on a long flight, locate the herd, come back here and tell us where they are to be found, and which way to go, so that Drift can be reunited with his family and friends.'

'Mmm, could be interesting at that, Mush. Any idea where they might be hiding out?'

'The Farley Enclosure, we think.'

'That's a long long way north.'

'We know that,' said Daisy, 'that's why we have come to the best flyer in the forest.'

'You are a clever whatchamacallit. I might be interested at that, I am in the business of long distance surveillance activities, you know, but it will cost you mind, and my services don't come cheap. Cheep cheep!'

'Mmm,' said Daisy, 'I had a feeling you might say that. How much, Bread n' Cheese?'

'What can you offer?'

'Well,' said Daisy, undoing the top pocket of his thick black coat, 'I do have this.'

Sparkling moonlight flashed from the strange object that Daisy now had in his right paw. He held it up to the moon and gently waved it around to make the best of the moonbeams.

'What is that?' whispered Drift.

'It's a ring, with a real diamond in the middle,' said Daisy proudly. 'A biggun too and harder than any woodpecker's beak.'

'I can see it's a ring, Mush,' said Bread n' Cheese, skipping gently from left to right, and then right to left on the cross beam above them, unable to contain his excitement. 'I am not really interested in diamond rings myself,' he said, feigning disinterest, 'but I do know a bird who is. Come to think of it, he's the same colour as you, Mush.'

'Thought you might,' said Daisy, grinning.

'I'll do it!' said Bread n' Cheese. 'I'll do it! Pay me now and I'll see you here at the same time tomorrow.'

'No, no, no, no, no,' said Daisy. 'I wasn't born in the cow muck, Bread n' Cheese. You know me better than that. You fly off now and find the herd, come back and give us exact directions, and then you will have your ring.'

'How do I know you will pay me?'

'Because…because…' said Daisy, desperately trying to think of a suitable reason.

'Because you are a goodger,' suggested Drift.

'Aye that's it!' shouted Daisy. 'I am a goodger, you know that, don't you Bread n' Cheese, and goodger's always honour their debts.'

'Well, all right then, just this once,' wittered the cuckoo-swallow. 'I'll be quite a while mind. Five hours to be precise. I will be back here in five hours.'

'We'll be waiting,' said Daisy. 'God speed, Bread n' Cheese, and good luck.'

'Good luck, Bread n' Cheese,' shouted Drift into the night, but by then the fat bird was already on the wing and heading north for the Farley Enclosure.

After he'd gone they sat together on the cold steps beneath the Wondering Cross.

'I like the ring,' said Drift.

'It's a real beauty.'

'Where did you get it?'

'Humanthings.'

'Thought as much. Did you steal it?'

Daisy flashed Drift a withering look. 'Course not, Drift. How could you think such a terrible thing?'

'Sorry, Daisy. So how did you get it?'

'There were two of them, a male and female, parked up beneath the trees at twilight. I was wandering around half asleep at the time, trying to find a decent feed, blathering about in the undergrowth when I first spotted them. They got out of the car and minute or so later he was kneeling down in front of her, strange kind of business if you ask me. Then I saw it, even in the twilight, the last rays of sunlight flashing from the diamond. The male humanthing offered it to the female, and she took it too. Then they went off hand in hand for a walk through the forest and I didn't think any more of it, when suddenly there was a fearsome row. The female thing was screaming at the male as if she had had a bad dinner. I confess I got interested again then and came back and watched the carry on. The male humanthing was running back to the car and she was chasing him, yelling like crazy, and then with one huge scream she threw the ring at him. I saw it turning over and over as it flew through the air, the diamond flashing like silver berries. It hit him on the back of the head and bounced down into the long grass. I could see quite plainly where it came to rest, clear as anything with my own eyes, but they couldn't, the fools. The next thing was they were crawling around in the mucky fallen holly leaves, searching for the ring, though of course they couldn't find it, nowhere near, not even in the right place, because humanthings, as we all know, are really quite stupid, they don't understand the ways of the forest at all, and as soon as it grew dark they gave up. So I sauntered over and casually picked it up. I was going to run to after them and drop it at their feet, but at that moment they were still screaming at one another and then they jumped into the car, slammed the doors, started the engine, and roared off in a cloud of filthy blue smoke. I have never seen them again since, which is why I still have it here,' and he held it up again to the moon for it to perform its magic. 'Beautiful isn't it?'

'It is that,' said Drift, 'I have never seen anything like it, and you don't mind giving it up?'

'Nope, not really, not if it gets you back with your kinfolk. A diamond ring is no good to me.'

Drift thought about that for a moment and then said, 'Is it so far, to the Farley Enclosure?'

'Good way,' said Daisy, 'I have only been that far away once before myself.'

'I am not sure I would fancy travelling all that way on my own.'

'I have been thinking about that,' said Daisy, 'and I've had an idea.'

'Go on,' said Drift.

'He's going to be away for five hours at least, Bread n' Cheese I mean, he said so, didn't he. That gives us time to hoppit back to the sett. You could have another top up feed, I could tell Grelda and all the others that we are going to be away for a few days so they are not worrying about us, then we could both have some dinner, get ourselves ready, and we could still be back here in good time before Bread n' Cheese gets back.'

'That's all very well,' said Drift, 'but I still don't fancy travelling such a long distance in the forest alone.'

'But that's the whole point, my four legged footling friend,' said Daisy, grinning, 'I'd come with you... if you want.'

'Oh would you, Daisy? That would be wonderful; you really are a goodger, you know that, don't you!'

The badger smiled and nodded his head. 'Come on then, that's settled, we'll aim for the sett, and no time to lose.'

They travelled quickly through the dark forest, retracing their steps back toward the badgers' homeland. As he often did, Daisy walked with his head facing the ground, as if he were permanently on the look out for juicy worms and other tasty morsels. Drift didn't walk that way at all, but kept looking about him, anxious to see and hear and learn about everything there was to know, ahead, behind, above, to one side, then the other, and it was he who spotted the creature blocking the path ahead.

'What on earth is that?' said Drift, coming to a standstill.

Daisy glanced up and peered down the track.

'Eh? Oh that's Arkady. He's a pig, and a mighty fine specimen at that.'

Drift's eyes widened. 'Ugly thing though isn't he.'

'Drift!' said a surprised Daisy. 'Beauty is in the eye of the beholder, I am sure his fellows think he is a grand creature. We can't all be slim and handsome… like us.'

Drift giggled and by then they were standing before the huge pig.

'Hello Arkady,' said Daisy. 'What are you doing here?'

The pig looked up from his busy work.

'Oh hello, Badge. If you must know, I am exercising my porcine rights.'

'Oh aye, and what are they exactly?'

'Pannage!'

'And what's that when it's at home?'

'Pannage my dear boy is the pigs' god-given right to be turned out into the forest during the last quarter of the year to munch up all the gorgeous corns. The horses, sweet creatures as we all know, but slightly on the delicate side, can't handle the tastiest of nuts. Upsets their constitutions, poor things, whereas we, with our super cooled, super charged bellies, are able, and I have to say, most willing, to accept nature's bounty. Put on weight before the winter, that's my motto. Put on weight before the winter, and if you take my advice, that skinny friend of yours needs to pay some attention in that area.'

'They are not corns,' said Daisy, 'but acorns.'

'Never use that word,' said Arkady, dismissively, shaking his head hither and thither.

'What word?' asked Daisy.

'Ache corns, that's what you said,' said the pig, 'and I hate all aches. Headache, backache, bellyache, toothache, and the worst of all, curly tail ache, they are all dreadful things sent to try us. I never used the Ache word. That's why I only ever call 'em corns.'

'Whatever you say,' said Daisy, glancing at a bemused Drift who had never experienced any of those aches, and especially the last one.

Daisy thought about it for a second. It was quite true, the humanthings did allow the pigs a free run of the forest toward the end of the year, but after that, they all mysteriously disappeared, the pigs that is, and rumours abounded of terrifying stories as to their eventual fate. Badger didn't know for sure the truth of it, but his keen nose told him that the aromas that often swept from the windows of the humanthings' cottages was a warning that only a fool would ignore.

'That's all very well,' said Daisy, 'but do you mind getting off the path so we can get by. We are on most urgent business.'

'Sorry, no can do, stripy,' said Arkady, his snout already buried again in the leaf litter searching for his next nut.

'It's all right,' said Drift, anxious to be on his way. 'We can get round all right,' as he leapt the bank and jumped into the woods.

'It's all right for you,' moaned Daisy, 'you are a much better jumper than me.'

'Come on,' said Drift, and he dangled his right hoof down the bank for Badger to grip with his claw, and in the next moment Drift heaved him up and into the forest proper.

'Ugly thing though wasn't he,' said Drift again, tittering.

'Suppose he was at that,' giggled Daisy. 'A little bit perhaps and a bit thick too.'

'I thought that as well,' said Drift, 'though I didn't like to say.'

An hour later they were back at the sett telling Grelda all the news. Time for a good feed all round, and then back outside into the darkness. Daisy was still in the sett saying his final goodbyes while Drift went on ahead a little way into a clearing where the last of the lush grass remained.

Drift sniffed the ground. It sure smelt good, though he wouldn't eat it.

Daisy emerged from the burrow and saw Drift staring down at the pasture. He had often seen the fawn gawping at the grass and wondered what was going through his mind. This time Daisy had an idea. He crept up behind Drift on tiptoe, he could move through the forest quite silently when he needed to, all the best forest creatures had mastered that craft, for they all knew their very life might depend on it one day. In the next moment he reached forward and grabbed the back of Drift's neck and thrust his head, face downwards, firmly into the pasture.

'Oi!' shouted Drift. 'Be careful! What did you go and do that for?'

And then something quite queer happened. Grass had entered Drift's mouth. Quite a bit of it too. It was all right; in fact it was better than all right. It was sweet and luscious and tasty and fresh and filling and in the next second Drift's mouth was moving about, almost by itself, ten to the dozen, as he began chewing the cud.

A moment later he turned and glanced across at his friend. The badger was standing up on his back feet grinning like a... like a... crazy badger.

'What are you giggling at?' asked Drift.

'At you,' said the badger. 'Thought you might need a little help in the feeding department, and it sure worked didn't it. After all, you can't rely on Grelda forever, especially when we are crossing the countryside toward the Farley Enclosure.'

Daisy was right, and Drift knew it too, though he didn't say.

'Feed for a while,' said Daisy, and then we'll be off. We don't want to miss Bread n' Cheese.'

Five

By the time they arrived back at the Wondering Cross it had begun to rain and worse than that, Bread n' Cheese wasn't there. No one was.

'He'll be back any minute,' said Daisy, sheltering under the right arm of the huge stone cross. 'Here,' he said, 'why don't you stand under the left arm?'

Drift did so but it didn't help much. He was wider than Daisy and the wind had stiffened and was blowing the rain this way and that. It had grown colder too and the moon was missing.

'Come on, Bread n' Cheese,' whispered Daisy, 'come along,' stamping his feet. 'Please do come along.'

'If he doesn't come soon,' said Drift, 'it will start getting light.'

Daisy didn't reply but he knew the fawn was right.

'What's that?' said a startled Drift.

He didn't have to wait for an answer because the grin on Daisy's face and the fierce wing beats from above told him that the cuckoo-swallow had finally returned.

'Shiver me timbers,' muttered the puzzled looking bird as he flapped his wings dry and began folding them away.

'Well?' said Daisy, impatiently.

'Listen Mush, you sent me on a wild goose chase, did you not?'

'Did I?'

Bread n' Cheese puffed out his cheeks and harrumphed.

'Well if only I had known.'

'Known what? Come on LTF, tell us all the news.'

'The reds are *not* in the Farley Enclosure. Definitely not! Searched everywhere I did, took me ages, and in the blinking rain too, I am telling you, it is not easy to fly in wet weather. You should try it some time. You ground dwelling lubbers have no idea what it is like trying to fly at night in the dark and rain. No comprehension at all.'

'I am sure it was most difficult,' sympathised Daisy. 'You didn't find the herd then?'

'Didn't say that! Didn't say that! Didn't say that!' said the cuckoo, not for the first time his voice stuck in repeat mode.

'Well?' said Daisy. 'Did you find them or not?'

'I met an old mate of mine.'

'Oh no,' murmured Daisy, cupping his paw round his snout and whispering from the side of his mouth to Drift who had come and stood beside him. 'Not another long and incredibly boring story.'

Bread n' Cheese narrowed his eyes and peered down. 'What did you say down there? What did you say?'

'Carry on, Bread n' Cheese. Please, please, get to the point.'

'I was trying to tell you all about it, but you kept interrupting. I met an old mate of mine called Ginger Beaks, he's a red kite you know, fine specimen of a bird, I was having a little rest on the telegraph wires at the time and he came by and of course we began chatting as you do, and I was telling him all about the big search for the reds and it was him who put me on to it.'

'Put you on to what?'

'The Black Woods.'

'What are the Black Woods?' whispered Drift.

'No idea,' said Daisy. 'Never heard of them, but no doubt he will tell us all about it eventually.'

'Beyond the Farley Enclosure, way beyond,' said Bread n' Cheese, 'that's where you will find the Black Woods. A cold and hostile place it is, where all the trees turn black. But there, beneath those cold and menacing trees I found them, and in big numbers too, camping they were, biggest gathering of reds I have seen for many a season. Quite impressive I have to say. All generations too, and it seemed as if they were having a gathering of some kind, a parlez, parlez, job.'

'And you are sure they were reds?' pressed Daisy.

'Positive Mush! They were making that stupid call of theirs, no offence young fella, ugly sound though it is, echoing through those dark black giants of trees, and you can't mix up the reds' calls with any other.'

'And you think they could be Drift's family?'

'Well I don't know that do I, but I am telling thee, it is perhaps the biggest herd I have ever seen, so there must be a good chance, though when I think about it, there was something different about it all.'

'In what way?'

'Hard to say really, it was almost as if they were preparing for a special journey or special event of some kind. I've not seen the like of it before.'

Daisy whispered across to Drift, 'Shall we pay him?'

Drift bobbed his head.

'Here you are, Bread n' Cheese,' shouted Daisy, and he slipped the ring from his pocket and fizzed it up to the dripping bird who caught it on the end of his beak. 'I am a badger of my word,' said Daisy, 'a goodger, as Drift would say.'

'Ooh ta, don't mind if I do,' and the bird slipped the ring over his toes and on to his ankle for safe keeping and carrying. 'I must be off now, things to do, places to see, a swallow's life is never dull.'

'Bye, Bread n' Cheese, and thank you,' they both called up into the night, as Bread n' Cheese heaved himself into the sodden darkness and flew away and then Drift said, 'He really does think he is a swallow.'

'Oh yes he does, always has. It gets really funny when the swallows actually return and he's right there, sidling up beside them and they think he's a little crazy. It's because he was raised by them of course. He doesn't know any different.'

'A bit like me and you,' said Drift.

Daisy sniffed the air. 'I don't think you will ever think you are a badger, do you? A little bit of a goodger may be, but never a badger. You will never forget your mother either, and anyway, the whole point of this little adventure is to return you to the big herd that sounds so impressive. Does it not? Is it not?'

Drift smiled with his eyes and bobbed his head.

'In that case we need to make a plan,' said Daisy.

'If you say so.'

'We have a long way to go. The plan is, we spend four hours on the move and four hours for rest and feeding and so on until we get there. That will mean travelling during the night and the day so we will have to keep our wits about us. There are different dangers in the forest during the hours of daylight. We must remain ever vigilant.'

'I agree,' said Drift. 'How long do you think it will take to get there?'

'About three days.'

That didn't sound so bad, thought Drift, and then he said, 'I didn't like the sound of the Black Woods much.'

Though he didn't like to say, neither did Daisy, for he had told a little white lie. He had heard of the Black Woods before, many times, and everything he had heard was evil.

'When shall we start?' said Drift, eager to begin.

Daisy stared up at the Wondering Cross and the jagged black sky beyond. The rain had stopped and the moon was struggling to be seen.

'Right now, my four legged friend, right now.'

Six

It was two hours later when Daisy coughed and said, 'In a few minutes we shall approach one of the humanthings' farms. This one is called Blue China Farm though I have no idea why. The thing is with farms, they can be extremely dangerous places.'

'How so?' asked Drift.

'Because,' answered Daisy, glancing about, 'because of the humanthings of course. They possess a truly dreadful machine.'

'What kind of machine?'

'The firing pipe. It brings great injury through the sky, and often, instant death. The humanthings use it without a second thought. It is truly unspeakable.'

'How does it work?'

'No one knows, but I warn you, Drift, if you see a humanthing with a firing pipe, you must leave the area as fast as you can.'

Drift shivered and nodded.

'And another thing,' said Daisy, 'the darn dogs.'

'Dogs have sold their souls,' said Drift, repeating what his mother had told him. 'Their bark is far worse than their bite. All noise and no dignity.'

Daisy guessed that his mother had told him that, though he didn't agree with it.

'Listen, young Drift. There are some dogs that will happily run and play with any forest creature all day long, but equally, there are dogs out there that would happily rip out your throat, and it is quite difficult to tell the two kinds apart. Remember this well: All dogs are descended from wolves, all of them, and they have never lost that wolf-like desire to kill, and eat. And size is no guide either. I have had fun and games with huge roly-poly dogs and I have come across those little whippersnapper terriers that are always spoiling for a fight to the finish. You mark my words, Drift, dogs are to be avoided, and if not that, treated with the greatest of suspicion.'

'I see,' said Drift, surprised at the turn of events.

'I don't blame the animals myself,' continued Daisy. 'It's the humanthings to blame, you can be sure of that. They train 'em you see, to be vicious killers, not all humanthings mind, and not all dogs are like that, but enough of them to make you most wary.'

'Thanks a lot,' said Drift, 'for putting me straight.'

Daisy smiled across at his young friend and patted his shoulder. 'Come on, it will be light soon and I'd like to be past the farm before the sun comes up.'

They set out with renewed vigour but hadn't been walking for more than five minutes when they heard a commotion on the track up ahead. Creatures were dashing this way and that across the path, frantically in and out of the woods as if they had been spooked.

'What's going on? What are they?' said Drift, pausing on the lane.

'Rabbits!' said Daisy. 'They are fine creatures, the rabbits, good friends, but something is up with them.'

A pretty female rabbit saw them and ran forward and stood before them, breathing heavily.

'Oh, we are so pleased to see you, Mister Badger. One of the young ones has caught his foot in a snare and the humanthings are coming! His mother is frightfully upset. Terrible state she is. You couldn't do anything to help could you? We'd be ever so grateful.'

'Show me, quick!'

'It's just down here, where the hazel trees border the paths, just beyond our burrows in the bank.'

Daisy set off at a fast pace as the rabbit glanced kindly at Drift who tagged along behind.

When they arrived at the snare it wasn't a pretty sight. A young rabbit had its front right paw caught fast in the wire trap. Tugging on the wire had only tightened the grip still further until the paw had begun to bleed. There was blood on the grass and it was mixing into the mud. The sorry looking youngster stared back at the extended gang that were now standing all around.

'It's no good!' said an older male rabbit with a torn ear. 'You will never get that snare open in a month of dandelion days. I've seen many a snare in my lifetime and I have never seen a rabbit escape from one yet.'

'All is not yet lost, Ripper,' said Daisy, closing in on the little one.

The big rabbit rolled his eyes. 'I'm telling you, it's hopeless. We shall all be in trouble if we are not careful. All we can do now is leave him to his fate. It's his own fault for standing in the trap in the first place, we must go now or we'll all be done for. Let's run back to the burrows.'

Hearing that, the little one's mother began wailing.

'We can't leave Riley, I simply won't leave him.'

In the distance, dogs barked.

'That's all we need,' said Ripper.

'I'll bite it off,' said Daisy.

'I've already tried that,' said Ripper, 'and with the greatest of respect, my teeth are much bigger than yours.'

'They might be bigger, Rips, but they are not harder, and they are not sharper, and you do not possess a set of jaws like these.' Daisy flashed his razor sharp teeth. Several of the young ones stood back in horror at the sight. 'Move away everyone, give me some room.'

'Try if you must,' said the big rabbit, 'but it will be a complete waste of time.'

Daisy snuggled up as close as he could to the young rabbit in order to set his jaws on the metal wire of the snare. Riley now looked dreadful, as if he had given up all hope.

The badger smiled at the rabbit and flexed his jaws. Then he began biting down. The wire was made of toughened steel and was incredibly hard. Daisy summoned all his strength and bit harder and harder and harder, and oddly while he was biting down he remembered his father from long ago doling out advice. 'Always look after your teeth, son,' he used to say, 'keep them clean and keep them sharp for one day they could save your life.'

The dogs were coming closer, their hideous barks echoing across the meadows and through the trees and every time they barked, the assembled creatures shivered and glanced over their shoulders. Daisy's whole head was now shaking violently at the effort of it as he bit harder than he had ever bitten before. Droplets of sweat formed on his forehead and tumbled down his snout.

In the background the pretty female rabbit said to Drift, 'I have never seen you round here before.'

'I haven't been this way before.'

'I think you and your friend are incredibly brave.'

'I have done nothing; it's all down to Daisy. He's the brave one.'

'I think you've got lovely eyes,' said the rabbit, peering into Drift's face.

Drift blushed. No one had ever told him he had a lovely anything before.

In the next moment everyone heard the loud snick as Daisy's teeth finally joined together through the wire. Everyone heard the ZING!!! As the wire broke and flew backwards like a coiled spring away from the young rabbit's paw.

'Well done!' screamed Riley's mother. 'He's free! He's free!'

'Hurray!' yelled the others.

'I have seen everything now,' said Ripper, 'I'd have wagered a year's supply of clover that that was impossible,' and then he shouted, 'Come along everyone! Back to the burrows before the dogs get you! Quick now! Hurry!'

Most of the rabbits dashed back to the safety of home, but Riley just lay there on the grass, his mother staring down at him.

'What's the matter with him?' she said frantically, first glancing at the youngster and then nervously back down the lane.

'Just a bit of shock I should think,' said Daisy, slapping Riley on his white tail and that stirred him to life, for he stood up and half hopped, half limped back toward the burrow, holding his cut paw clear of the muddy ground, drops of blood spattering the grass.

'Trouble's coming,' said Ripper, as he frantically tried to round up the last of the young ones. They could all see the dogs and humanthings now; they watched in horror as two men stooped and unclipped the leads. The dogs were running free.

'I think we'd better get out of here,' said Daisy. 'We don't want to meet up with that lot.'

'Come by again, won't you!' shouted the female rabbit to Drift, before she turned and gracefully hopped back toward the bank.

'Thank you so much,' said Ripper, 'offering Daisy his paw. 'For everything you've done.'

There was just enough time for a quick paw-shake and one last glimpse down the path at the closing dogs.

'Into the woods, Drift,' yelled Daisy. 'Hurry now!'

'I can smell a stream,' said the fawn, 'we'll head for the water and run through it to mask the scent.'

'You are a clever thing,' said Daisy, and already they were in the cover of the woodland.

'Will they catch us up?' said Drift, breathing heavily.

'I think not,' said Daisy, glancing back over his shoulder, for all the dogs had now arrived at the burrows and were desperately sniffing around this way and that in the vain hope of finding a straggler or two, greedily licking up any blood they could find. But by that time all the rabbits were safely tucked up far below ground, where even the humanthings with all their terrifying machines could not touch them. This time the rabbits had won the day, and they knew it.

'Looks like we've made it,' said Drift trotting ahead through the water, splish-splashing as they went.

'Seems that way,' said Daisy, 'and thank goodness for that.'

They slowed to a walking pace but when Drift glanced ahead again, there it was. A huge dog was standing in the stream before them, staring straight at them. It was brown and black with a low-slung belly. Its mouth was open and it slobbered into the water, all the while displaying its ferocious teeth. It was no more than twenty paces in front of them and it was walking directly toward them, slowly, but with the clear intent of the mischief it had in mind.

'Trouble!' said Drift. 'Big trouble!'

Daisy peered ahead. 'Oh my giddy aunt!'

Drift glanced to one side. There was what looked like a disused foxhole on top of which, an old oak tree had long since fallen down, but the entrance was still partly exposed.

'On the right,' whispered Drift. 'A hole, you get yourself down there to safety.'

'But what about you? I can't leave you alone to face that brute.'

'I'll be all right,' said Drift. 'I'll try and outrun it. All that green grass has put some spring into my step.'

The dog was still confidently approaching, as if weighing up which of the interlopers to attack first.

'SNIFFLES!' yelled one of the humanthings from back by the burrows.

The dog stopped and glanced that way. Drift and Daisy stood perfectly still. The dog barked. It was trying to summon help.

'SNIFFLES! You come here, you stupid dog, or I'll murder ya!' bellowed the vile man through the trees.

The dog half smiled at Drift and Daisy and slowly nodded its head as if to say: You have been very lucky this time, but if I ever see you near my farm again, I'll have you, I'll have you, you see if I don't.

Daisy couldn't resist a little dismissive wave at the dog as it growled and turned tail and ran away back toward its loudmouthed master.

'What did I tell you?' said Drift, grinning. 'All noise and no dignity.'

Daisy giggled. 'Phew, that was close, we were lucky there.'

'Yes,' agreed Drift, 'we were, a bit,' wondering whether he could really have outrun such an impressive beast.

'Sniffles!' said Daisy, mockingly, 'what a ridiculous name.'

'A ridiculous name for a ridiculous dog,' added Drift.

'That's true. Now come on, while they are still busy over by the burrows, we can hurry down to the farm and skirt the main buildings and be safely on the other side before they even realise we have been that way.'

'Good idea,' said Drift, as they trotted from the stream and cut back toward the track that would take them down close by Blue China Farm.

Seven

The sun was fully up as they approached the farm but everything about was quiet. The cows had been milked and had been put out in the meadow that ran all the way up the hill beyond the barns. The only sign of life was an old cat busy mousing in the farm courtyard and it was so keen on its business it didn't spot the strangers tip toeing past the gates.

'Easy-peasy,' whispered Daisy, as they reached the end of the ancient redbrick buildings. The lane forked there, the left one going on up the hill, while the other way turned sharply to the right at the end of the cowsheds.

'Come on,' said Daisy, 'I hate this place. It doesn't smell right to me.'

'Are you sure this is the right way?' asked Drift.

'Yes, I think so,' said Daisy. 'I am sure it is.'

At the end of the buildings they turned right, hoping to scoot away as fast as possible, but there, standing immediately in front of them, gaping at them, was a humanthing.

Drift gulped.

'Oh dear,' said Daisy, looking uncharacteristically guilty.

'Hello Mister Badger,' said the humanthing.

Drift's eyes almost fell from his head. He eased closer to the badger and whispered, 'It spoke to you.'

'I know. I heard. I can't believe it. That has never happened before.'

'And who's your young friend then?' it continued.

'Oh… yes… this is Drift,' said Daisy. 'We are on our way to the Farley Enclosure and the Black Woods beyond.'

The humanthing giggled. 'Well you are going the wrong way, stripy pants.'

'It's a young one,' whispered Drift. 'A humanthing fawn.'

'Of course it's a young one,' said Daisy, 'it's only as big as me for goodness sake. Female, if I am not much mistaken.'

'Do you think it has a firing pipe?' whispered Drift.

'Course not, look at it. They don't trust the tiny ones with firing pipes. Even *they* are not that stupid.'

They both took a long second long look at the grinning creature before them for they couldn't quite believe what they were seeing, and hearing. It was true; the young female humanthing was only as tall as the badger and it did speak. It had spoken to them as clear as day. They looked it directly in the eye, and the humanthing's eyes were a very strange bright blue, like the sky on a hot summer's day. Furthermore, its face was soft looking and white with just a hint of pink on the cheeks, and the phizog was surrounded by curly, light coloured hair of a texture similar to the horses' tails. It was clothed in some kind of short blue dress, which frankly, Daisy considered quite ridiculous, and from there, its stubby white legs stretched down to some hideous thick blue shoes.

It was a well-known fact that the humanthings always wore clothes; Daisy had rarely seen one without them, and not only that, they often forced their dogs and horses to wear clothes too. How truly absurd.

'You say we are going the wrong way?' said Daisy.

'You are if you want the Farley Enclosure and the Black Woods beyond. It's thataway, up the hill,' and the young humanthing pointed up the track.

'Thank you,' said Drift. 'Thank you very much.'

'You are most welcome.'

'Do you have a name?' asked Daisy.

'Of course I have a name.'

'And it is?'

'I am Helena. I am very pleased to meet you,' and it offered Daisy its plump paw.

Daisy took it, and squeezed it. It was soft and hairless and smelt of phoney flowers. In all his days he had never touched a humanthing before, in fact he had never had the urge to do so, but then again he had never spoken to a humanthing before either.

'And tell me,' said Daisy, warming to the strange occasion, 'have you always been able to speak to the animals?'

'Oh yes,' it said in a squeaky voice, 'always, even before I learnt to speak to my own kind.'

'How most peculiar,' said Daisy.

'Yes, isn't it. I tell my parents I can talk to the creatures all the time, but they just laugh at me.'

'I'm sure they do.'

'I speak to the fairies too you know.'

Drift and Daisy shared a look of bewilderment.

'Really? Can you?' said Daisy, disbelievingly, for though he had heard countless stories of fairies in the forest since he was a tiny wee thing, he had never actually seen one, nor knew anyone else that had.

'Oh yes,' it continued, 'there are a few fairies round here, but mainly they live up in the Black Woods, where you are going.'

'Really?'

'What's a fairy?' whispered Drift.

'I'll tell you later,' said Daisy from the side of his mouth.

'Ask it why it's called Blue China Farm?' muttered Drift.

'You ask it,' said Daisy. 'You are not dumb.'

So Drift did.

'That's easy,' the thing said, 'because we eat all our meals off Blue China, silly boys.'

'And you eat meat?' said Drift.

'Of course we eat meat, every day. Doesn't everyone? Don't you eat meat?'

'Certainly not!' said Drift, 'I've never had the desire, dreadful habit if you ask me. Dreadful!'

The humanthing appeared puzzled at Drift's answer and by his hostile tone and turned to Daisy. 'Don't you eat meat, Mister Badger?'

'Well um, not really, no, oh, not often, mmm,' stuttered Daisy, glancing guiltily at Drift. 'Perhaps occasionally on very special days, but not really, no, I can live without it, err, I don't normally need to eat meat.'

The truth was that Badger could not do without his meat. True, generally it consisted of fat juicy worms, but he would have eaten that hamburger he took back to Grelda if she hadn't wanted it, and heaven forbid, and he would never tell this to Drift, but he had also been known to clean up some of the night-time casualties on the highway, before the greedy foxes and magpies could beat him to it. Yes, an occasional fresh rabbit or pheasant or squirrel, just now and again mind, made a very welcome addition to any badger's diet, though he wouldn't like the rabbits to know that, and he'd certainly never kill one, never, and in his own eyes, that made it all right. He was simply performing a public service, cleaning up the mess. Daisy turned back to the humanthing. 'Well, we must be off now; it's been so nice to meet you.'

'And you too. Bye, bye.'

Drift and Daisy retraced their steps and turned on to the track that led up the hill.

'Be very careful in the Black Woods!' the humanthing screamed after them. Daisy glanced back and waved again and the last thing he saw was the little female running back into the courtyard in that jerky unstable running style that all young humanthings adopt, as if it takes them years and years to learn to run, which in fact it does, which just goes to show once again how terribly backward they really are in so many ways. Fancy it taking several years to learn to run properly, for goodness sake. Drift taught himself to canter in twenty-five minutes and how clever was that?

Back on the lane they reached the brow of the hill and gazed down at the valley beyond. There was one further large field that clearly belonged to the farm in which fifty assorted cows and sheep were hard at it, grazing away. At the end of the field was a wooden fence and beyond that, mixed open countryside. They would be back in the forest once they crossed the fence, the borderline, and they would feel a heck of a lot happier and safer when they were.

'Come on,' said Daisy, 'we need to find somewhere safe where we can rest up a while.'

They increased the pace and were at the gate in no time. Daisy demonstrated how humanthings' gates were so easy to open and close once you knew the magic tricks involved. Drift watched intently, remembering everything there was to see.

Once back in forest territory Drift said, 'So what is a fairy?'

Daisy smiled and shook his head. 'A mythical creature.'

'What does that mean?' asked Drift. 'Mythical.'

'A mythical creature is…' Daisy paused and stared at the sky as he tried to sort out his mixed up thoughts. 'A creature that other creatures believe exists, though they have never actually seen one. You follow?'

'I think so,' said Drift, when in fact he was more confused than ever. 'And what do they look like.'

'Never seen one,' said Daisy, 'but they say they look like small humanthings… with wings.'

'With wings?' said Drift, unable to stifle a belly laugh.

'Yes,' insisted Daisy, 'and you can see right through them.'

'You can see right through them?' repeated Drift, stifling a heavy laugh this time through his nostrils.

'Don't keep repeating everything I say,' said Daisy, just about keeping the annoyance from his words. 'You'll recognise them when you see them. That's for sure.'

'And they live in the Black Woods?'

'So Helena said, you heard it, along with the big herd of reds, and if we are really lucky, your uncle Mo as well.'

For the moment Drift had forgotten all about his uncle Mo, and the real reason for their journey in the first place, but Daisy's mention of him brought all kinds of strange images to his mind. A huge king stag in a clearing waggling his antlers this way and that, a stag surrounded by armies of see-through fairies with wings, all singing and dancing.

'This Black Woods sounds like some crazy place,' said Drift.

'Yep, it sure does,' said Daisy, pushing back some browning bracken. 'Here,' he said, it's safe and quiet in here. Let's rest up for a while before we move on.'

Drift lay down and promptly fell asleep and dreamed dreams the like of which he had never dreamt before. Daisy slept fitfully, worrying of where they going, and what was to come.

Eight

Drift was the first to wake and he wondered why, though he didn't immediately open his eyes. He swivelled his ears and listened. Birds were singing, Daisy was snoring, and far away a tractor was puffing and huffing up and down a hill. He detected no danger warnings, no sounds of movement close by, but something was not right. It made him feel uneasy. He sniffed the air. There was danger there, real danger that he didn't immediately understand. Then it came to him.

Smoke!

There are three things all forest creatures are instinctively afraid of: humanthings, that goes without saying, wild wolves, and it made no difference that there hadn't been a wild wolf in the forest for nigh on three hundred years, the fear of that predatory beast still ran strongly in the genes, and lastly... fire.

Smoke meant fire, and fire is terrible. Drift opened his eyes and stood upright and sniffed the wind. It was coming from the north, the very way they wished to travel.

'Daisy, wake up!'

Daisy grunted, but resumed his snoring.

Drift closed on the badger and delivered a decent kick to his rump.

'Oi! Eh! What are you doing?' moaned Daisy, as he staggered to his feet, rubbing his eyes and staring at Drift. 'What did you do that for?'

Drift nodded to the north. 'Smoke. Fire.'

The badger sniffed the wind.

'I can't smell anything.'

'I am telling you, there is a fire, and it is coming this way.'

Daisy snorted again, filling his lungs with a huge breath.

'There might be the slightest whiff, I'll give you that, but I shouldn't think it was anything worth worrying about.'

'I am telling you, Daisy, it's a *big* fire and it's moving quickly…toward us.'

'And it's coming from the north, you say?'

Drift nodded, glancing nervously back that way.

'The way we want to go,' said Daisy.

'Yes. Precisely. So what are we going to do now?'

'Well normally with fire the natural thing to do is run as fast as you can in the opposite direction. But fire is so unpredictable; the wind can swing it round in an instant. You have to be so careful with it. You should never play with fire, Drift, never.'

'But if we go back the way we came we shall never reach the Black Woods.'

'Yes, my thoughts exactly. I'll tell you what we'll do; we'll head toward it and inspect it for ourselves. Once we can see it with our own eyes then we can make a plan as to what to do next.'

'But isn't that dangerous?' said Drift.

'Yes, it could be. You are right. But have you any better ideas?'

Drift had to admit that he did not and they set out across the clearing northward towards the increasing smell of the smoke.

The fawn did see the piece of curled up rope on the grass but for some reason stood on it anyway. In the next moment the rope was wiggling and wriggling and writhing and wrapping itself around Drift's front hoof. The fawn panicked.

'What the blinking heck!'

Daisy stood back and started laughing.

'You have stood on poor Adrian! You dope!'

The rope, or whatever it was, was now speaking too, addressing Drift, and it was not happy.

'Oi! What did you do that for? Clumsy feet!'

'Oh, I am terribly sorry; I thought you were a piece of old rope.'

'Old rope indeed! Do I look like old rope? You are very lucky I didn't bite you!'

'Hello Adrian,' said Daisy, still grinning, 'this is my friend Drift. He has never met a snake before. An honest mistake, my friend, I do hope you will forgive the fawn.'

'Well…' said the snake begrudgingly. 'I might. But he woke me up!'

'He's an adder,' explained Daisy, 'and his bite is poisonous. It can be quite serious too, though I don't think Adrian has ever bitten anyone in anger, have you Ade?'

'I could do though!' said the snake, still glaring up at Drift, still angry that he had been wakened.

'You better get away, Mister Snake,' said Drift. 'There's a big fire on the way.'

Adrian yawned and tasted the air with his tongue.

'So what if there is, so what?' and he settled down again into a tight circle.

'Aren't you going to hurry away?' asked a puzzled Drift. 'For if you don't, you could end up as roasted snake.'

Adrian yawned again and that made Daisy yawn.

'My family have lived in this precise part of the forest for hundreds of years and if we ran away every time there was a piffling fire, then where would we be? I ask you. In trouble, that's where. I have no intention of running from some fiddling fire. There is a blaze every year, sometimes more than one. I am safe enough here. We all are.'

'But where will you go?'

The snake nodded to the bank beyond.

'See that bank; see that hole, see that tunnel, well it travels deep beneath the ground. There isn't a fire imaginable that could ever reach us down there. We have never lost a member of our family to fires in my lifetime and we shall not be starting today.'

And with that Adrian straightened himself out and lolloped away in a truly funny fashion toward the tunnel and disappeared, its tail waggling provocatively in the entrance before it finally vanished.

'I wish we could do that,' said Drift.

'As a matter of fact, my friend,' said Daisy, grinning, 'I can.'

'You are not going to leave me are you?'

'No Drift, of course not. Now didn't we say we were going to go and inspect this fiery beast?'

Drift nodded, glancing to the north and back at Daisy.

'Well come on then.'

They set out at a good pace. The stink of smoke was much stronger now and on the horizon black clouds could be seen drifting into the sky.

'It's a biggun,' said Daisy.

'I told you that ages ago.'

Suddenly they heard the thunder of hooves. Horses were approaching. They burst from the cover of the trees; their eyes wide open and panicked. Drift thought they looked terrified.

'Away! Away!' cried the leading horse. 'Fire! Fire! Save yourselves!'

Twelve horses thundered by, running this way and that, spooked and frightened, seemingly unable to control their direction, and totally unable to comprehend why the stupid fawn and the equally stupid badger were heading directly in the opposite direction, toward the flames.

Drift and Daisy could see red and yellow flashes now, rushing up silver birch saplings, destroying everything in their path. A solitary pig appeared, a large pink sow, and it waddled by, trying as hard as it could to appear unconcerned, but the look in its eyes told a different story. Its eyelashes had been singed. It didn't speak, not a word, just nodded over its shoulder at the approaching fire, as if the simple badger and his peculiar pal hadn't seen it at all.

Daisy spotted a small mound ahead and dashed up it and once on the top stood high on his back legs and peered toward the inferno. Drift joined him; there being just enough space for the two of them to stand together.

'My goodness, just look at that!'

Together they gazed out across the countryside. As far as they could see from left to right the forest was on fire, thick smoke rising urgently and fleeing into the air in one solid bank of swirling fumes. At the base of the smoke were orange and red flickers, like giant lizards' tongues, spreading their evil, terrifying all the creatures in its path, destroying everything.

'It really is a biggun,' said Daisy, 'a huge one in fact.'

'I can see that,' said Drift, nervously, 'but what do we do now? We have to get through that somehow. We have to get to the other side.'

'Yes we do,' smirked Daisy knowingly, tapping his muzzle, 'and I know just how we can do it.'

'How?'

'The railway.'

'The what?'

'The railway, I said.'

'What's a railway?'

'Come on, I'll show you.'

Daisy set out to the left at a fair pace with Drift catching up as the badger explained that a railway was like a highway, but the vehicles ran on fixed silver tracks. In the summertime the tracks turned hot in the sunshine and it wasn't unknown for unwary creatures to take a nap on the cosy rails, and that was very dangerous indeed.

'You must never, ever, pause on the railway, Drift. Never. Understand?'

Drift nodded again though he wasn't entirely sure why, and then he said, 'But what I don't understand is how the railway will take us through the wall of fire.'

'You'll see. You'll see.'

In front of them now was a big mound, much higher and thicker than the last one, like a huge grass wall running across the countryside.

'Now what?' asked a puzzled Drift.

'That's it,' said Daisy, 'that's the railway.'

'But where is it?'

'It runs along the top.'

'But won't the flames just run up and over it?'

'Yes they will, but not through here, come on.'

Daisy ran ahead again with Drift trotting behind and then the fawn saw what Daisy was talking about. There was a vast hole through the middle of the embankment, and already sheltering in the hole under the railway was a drove of donkeys, eight of them all told.

They turned about as one and gaped at the strangers.

Then the biggest one, a mean looking grey and black old brute said, 'You want to share our bridge?'

'Yes please,' said Daisy, as Drift stood behind him, 'if you don't mind.'

'I don't know yet whether I mind or not. What can you offer us in return?'

What could they offer the donkeys in return? It was a good question. Fact was they had nothing of value, and certainly nothing of interest to a drove of dopey donkeys.

'Yes, come along,' said one of the bossy females, pushing her way to the front. 'We were here first and it's only fair that you make a contribution. If you can't offer something of value, you can jolly well push off! It's our bridge after all. We found it first.'

'I know something of value,' said Drift.

Daisy peered at him quizzically.

'And what would you know?' said the big donkey, glaring down his nose at the fawn.

'I know where there is luscious feed to be had.'

'Oh yeah,' said the brute, clearly not believing Drift.

'Where?' said the females, as one, and they all took a step toward Drift and began nuzzling him. 'Where, where, where?'

'It's been left outside Blue China Farm. In the road where the lane forks.'

'I know of that place,' said the mean looking male, 'where the young humanthing can actually speak.'

'That's it!' said Daisy, picking up the story. 'That's the one.'

'Why would they leave feed outside? It doesn't make any sense.'

'No idea,' said Drift, 'all I know is, I took my fill,' and he burped loudly to reinforce the point. 'And there was lots left after I'd finished.'

The male turned and gazed at the others and there was a fair bit of muttering between them.

'I think we should investigate this, don't you?'

'Oh, yes, yes, yes, for sure.'

There followed considerable nodding and pawing of the ground and then suddenly all the females bared their teeth and began braying together in a stupid high-pitched voice, not quite a rendition of the traditional hee-haw, but close enough, 'Oh yes! Oh yes! Oh yes!'

'Come on then,' ordered the big brute, licking its lips. 'We'd better go and see,' and it moved away in the direction that Drift and Daisy had come from, the females trotting excitedly behind.

'Watch out for the dogs!' Daisy yelled after them.

The leader turned his head and bellowed over his shoulder. 'I am not afraid of any damn dog! Kick 'em hard, that's my motto. Kick 'em hard! Don't you know that a donkey's kick is the fiercest kick in the whole of the forest? Don't you know anything at all? I've never seen a dog yet who could bite me with a broken jaw.'

The donkeys brayed in unison and disappeared as Drift said, 'Is it true, what it said about its kick?'

'Pretty much, you don't ever want to be kicked by a donkey. Especially a mad one like him.'

'I wonder what they will think when they find there is no free feed.'

'I don't know,' said Daisy, 'but I don't want to be anywhere near them when they discover it. That male looked a mean bag of rotten bones to me. Come on, let's see how the fire is raging,' and they turned and hurried under the bridge to take a better look.

The wind had changed and was now blowing in their faces, forcing the smoke toward the embankment and through the underpass. Drift began coughing.

'It'll soon clear away,' said Daisy, without much conviction.

The flames were hurtling toward the embankment, urged on by the wind. Some gorse bushes nearby went up in a matter of seconds, the ancient central stems crackling and spitting as they burnt in spurts of flame. The red-hot tongues were now at the base of the embankment. Daisy and Drift took a few paces back to the safety of the centre of the underpass as the flames began leaping up the embankment, burning everything in its path, ragwort, brown bracken, a young apple tree, hazel bushes, abandoned birds' nests, all succumbing to the rampant destruction of the feverish blaze.

Once on the top of the embankment the fire would not be stopped by a few metal tracks. It paused for a second or two at the steel rails, waiting for a gust of wind to blow sparks across into the dried grass on the other side.

Whoosh!

It had set alight again and in the next moment the blaze was sweeping down the other side.

'See,' said Daisy, as they went to inspect the north side, the way they wanted to go, 'I told you I could get us through the fire. It's not so difficult when you know how.'

'You are so clever, Daisy, I'd never have thought of that.'

'Wisdom comes to us all in time, Drift; you will gather it sooner than you think.'

They stood together and gazed out across the blackened earth.

Ahead of them were smouldering ruins of destroyed heather, gorse bushes rendered to charcoal, larger trees blackened and still smoking. The stench was terrific. All the grass and feed had been ruined for weeks to come, but worse than that, it was still red-hot to the touch, impossible to walk on.

Ramble Bang! Ramble Bang! Ramble Bang! Ramble Bang!

Drift ducked his head. 'What on earth is that?'

'Oh that,' said Daisy, glancing up at the brick roof from where old cobwebs now rained down. 'That's the train going over the top, the cars running on the steel tracks I was telling you about.'

'Such as dreadful noise,' said Drift. 'Hideous!'

'It's soon gone,' said Daisy. 'It can't hurt you so long as you don't go near it.'

And he was right, though for some time afterwards the underpass echoed and vibrated to the noise of the crossing train. When it had gone they glanced back out at the smouldering destruction.

'It'll be ages before we can travel on that,' said Drift, impatient to get started.

Daisy glanced at the sky.

'May be not.'

It was as if the Great Stag in the heavens himself had been watching and had witnessed their plight, and had ordered instant relief. The dark clouds began spitting and in the next moment a heavy downpour teemed toward the blackened earth. The countryside began hissing like a million snakes and steaming as the water confronted the smouldering fires.

'That was lucky,' said Daisy, as the heavy shower swept across the land.

'Was it just luck, though?' asked Drift.

'What do you mean?'

Drift shrugged his shoulders and placed his front hooves on to the dampened grass.

'I think I can manage it now,' said Drift, 'can you?'

'Don't see why not,' said Daisy, 'anything you can do, I can do too. I shall walk in your footsteps.'

Drift tiptoed through the ashes and charcoal, Daisy close behind, their eyes fixed on the thick woods on the horizon that had escaped the worst of the blaze. Now they were more determined than ever to reach their goal.

Nine

Ahead of them was another fence and within the fence a five-bar gate. Next to the gate, fixed on the fence, was a roughly made square sign painted in bright red on a white background. The sign still boasted the chemical stink of fresh paint.

'What does it say?' asked Drift.

'No idea,' said Daisy. 'I have never learnt the humanthings' magic of reading. Not many of the forest creatures have. Grelda said she could read and I took her newspapers back when they blew through the forest, usually after the humanthings had departed. But one day I saw her studying one, and the pictures were all upside down, so I don't really think she can read at all. Langley the owl says he can read and I imagine he probably can, a little, but he's not here to help today. But it makes no odds, you don't need to be able make out those words to realise that this isn't a welcoming sign.'

They both stared back at the vile red picture that had been painted above the letters. It consisted of an ugly humanthing skull and beneath that were two large bones placed one across the other.

'It's horrid,' said Drift.

'It's more than horrid,' said Daisy, 'it's enough to give anyone nightmares.'

Daisy traced the letters with his paw. F…A…R…L…E…Y E…N…C…L…O…S…U…R…E.. the top line said, followed by K…E…E…P……O…U…T…while the bottom line in slightly smaller, underlined letters said: T…R…E…S…P…A…S…S…E…R…S…. W…I…L…L…. B…E…… S…H…O…T

'One thing is for sure,' repeated the badger, 'it is not a welcome sign.'

'So what do we do now?' asked Drift.

Daisy opened the gate.

'We go on of course, it's our forest as much as theirs, and we have no choice if we want to reach the Black Woods.'

'If you say so,' said Drift.

'I do say so,' insisted Daisy, closing the gate behind them.

The Farley Enclosure was a huge area of open countryside dotted with copses and small woods throughout its territory. The pasture was lush and much sought after and nasty notices or not, there were plenty of courageous creatures grazing there, horses, donkeys, rabbits, hares, cattle, pigs, not to mention the myriad of fat feathered friends who waddled up and down, though most of them were inclined to stay close to the large lake known as the Hangman's Pool. Daisy had been there before a long time ago, though he still felt uneasy as they walked briskly through the trees.

Out of nothing they heard three loud bangs coming from up ahead. Drift stood bolt still and swivelled his ears, his nose frantically twitching, trying to catch any information that might be carried on the oncoming wind.

'Firing pipes,' whispered Daisy. 'Big danger! Humanthings up ahead that's for sure. Up to no good, no doubt about it. We must be extra careful.'

'There are four or five of them,' said Drift, still peering straight ahead.

'You can tell all that?' asked a mighty impressed Daisy.

'Oh yes,' smiled Drift. 'And dogs too. Little dogs I should say, yappers, perhaps five or six of them.'

Daisy made a strange noise through his nose. 'Hoooh!'

'What do you mean?' asked Drift.

'I mean wherever humanthings are to be found in numbers you can bet your stubby little tail there will always be trouble.'

'My tail is not so stubby,' giggled Drift. 'Have you seen your own lately?'

Crazily Daisy turned round as if to check on his own tail before thinking better of it.

'I think we'll have to skirt away to the right and go round by Hangman's Pool. We don't want to meet that lot if we can avoid it.'

'Whatever you say,' said Drift, 'you are the expert.'

They crept away to the right, keeping their heads down, while increasing the pace, but it made little difference, the noise of the humanthings' firing pipes grew louder and louder, and the excitable dogs could be heard quite clearly now. To Drift and Daisy it seemed as if they were deliberately following them, and then a dreadful notion entered Daisy's mind. Perhaps they were out hunting. Perhaps they were hunting for badgers and deer. It wouldn't be the first time, though he didn't dare tell Drift of his dark thoughts. Daisy shivered again and muttered, 'Come on Drift, this is bad. I don't like it at all.'

In the next moment a huge black horse bolted from the copse up ahead. Perched on top of the horse was a fat red-faced male humanthing wearing a most silly black hat. It looked faintly ridiculous, the humanthing, and most uncomfortable, bouncing up and down, all wobbly belly and bloated red face, and for a moment Daisy let out a pitying laugh. They watched transfixed as it closed on them. They saw it take a horn from the side of the horse and listened as it blew a dreadful sound across the forest like a drunken owl.

'What is it doing?' whispered Drift, too scared to move.

'Making a complete spectacle of itself as per usual,' said Daisy, his arms folded nonchalantly across his chest.

The horse and rider veered away to the left and in the next moment five walking humanthings came from the forest in a line abreast, a good distance between each. They were all armed with firing pipes and sticks that they used to beat the undergrowth, calling and shouting and laughing all the while.

'They are after the birds,' whispered Daisy. 'They often chase the bigger birds, ducks, pheasants, partridges, that kind of thing. Makes their lives a nightmare, it does.'

At that exact moment three pheasants came in swooping low over their heads. The humanthings pointed their firing pipes to the sky and let go a volley of shot. Drift's ears shivered violently at the noise. Feathers fluttered down, freshly skimmed from one of the terrified birds.

'That one's been hit,' said Drift, nodding at the sky.

'Aye, and he won't be the last one today,' said Daisy, and just as he said that, a pheasant fell sharply from the sky and bounced three times heavily on the heather, before coming to rest not ten yards from where they stood.

'Come on,' said Daisy, jumping into a run. 'Follow me, Drift. We must get away!'

But it was too late.

The line of humanthings had spotted the deer and the badger running away to their left. Movement attracts the eye, it always does.

'Look at that!' called out one.

'I am having a go at that!' yelled a second. 'It's too good an opportunity to miss!'

In the next moment the firing pipes were sending their red-hot messages of death searing through the forest.

Bang! Bang! Bang!

Thundering shot hurtled after them through the trees.

'Blimmin heck!' yelled Daisy.

'I don't like it!' shouted Drift, spooked now and sprinting on ahead, 'I don't like it at all!'

A second volley of fire ripped through the golden leaves, tearing twigs haphazardly from the trees, slamming into half asleep oak trees. They would not be happy at that, not at all.

'Behave yourselves!' screamed Daisy over his shoulder, though he knew it was a complete waste of time because these stupid humanthing creatures would never understand him in a month of honey hives.

A third volley ripped after them, noise and smell and smoke and danger. Daisy crouched down startled in the cover of crumpled bracken and when he next looked up he saw Drift falling awkwardly to the turf.

Drift, his friend, had been shot.

Ten

'Oh no!' yelled Daisy, as he leapt from the undergrowth.

At that moment five more fat pheasants came flying over like miniature aeroplanes, startled and out of control. For a moment they distracted the humanthings and in the next second they were all firing frantically into the grey sky.

Daisy reached Drift. The fawn was lying still on the grass and the badger feared the worst. He had witnessed many times what fearful injuries firing pipes could produce.

'Drift! Drift!' he said. 'Are you all right?'

The fawn lifted his head from the turf and said: 'I have been hit.'

'Whereabouts?'

'Back leg... I think.'

'You rest there a moment,' said Daisy, rushing to inspect the back legs and the damage.

Drift was right. He had been hit, but he had also been incredibly lucky. The shot had smashed into him on the bottom corner of his young hoof and had blown a small portion of it away. The force of the blow had knocked Drift clean off his feet.

'It's not so bad,' soothed Daisy. 'You've been hit on the hoof, that's all. Blown a little away, but it will soon grow back. You've been quite fortunate. You've been lucky this time. Can you stand up?'

'I think so,' said Drift, struggling to his feet.

The noise of the firing pipes was growing dimmer now, though the yelping of dogs was still evident.

'I think they are going away,' said Daisy, sniffing the wind.

'I don't think I can go much further today,' whimpered Drift.

'You stay here,' said Daisy, 'I have seen something up ahead that just might help.'

Drift lay down again and flattened his ears to his head as his mother had trained him to do, always when resting show a low profile to the world; she used to say, as Daisy rushed away into a nearby section of thicker woodland.

The thing that had attracted the badger's attention was a vast ancient oak that had fallen down many moons before. Most of the branches had long since rotted away, but the fat trunk lying on its side looked kind of inviting, for there was a gaping hole on the near side.

Daisy cautiously entered for you never knew what dangers might lurk inside a potential tree home. The year before he had found a similar fallen tree, an ancient yew that one was, and on that occasion he'd rushed inside to be faced with a prone humanthing, a stinking old man surrounded by green poison bottles. The surprise of it had frightened Daisy to the tips of his claws, and it didn't help when the long whiskered humanthing had snarled at him and launched an empty green bottle that glanced off the side of Daisy's bonce. It had been a close call and he'd never forget it, and he had no wish to repeat the experience.

The space inside the fallen oak was surprisingly large. The entire centre of the tree had been eaten away by generations of ants and wasps and heaven knows what else. It was warm in there too and somehow it smelt welcoming, and safe. Daisy trotted back to Drift to tell him of his find.

'Come on,' he said, 'we'll be safe and sound inside the tree. You can sleep for the rest of the day. Build up your strength for tomorrow.'

Drift limped awkwardly behind Daisy until he was standing outside the fallen monster. His leg didn't really hurt, may be a little numb, it just felt kind of strange to be standing and walking on a slightly jagged hoof, though he knew he would soon get used to it, and as Daisy had said before, the hoof would quickly grow back.

'Come on in,' said Daisy, eager to show his friend the extent of their newfound accommodation.

Drift followed him inside.

Daisy could see from the expression on the fawn's face that he approved. The ground was covered in fresh undisturbed moss and was beautifully soft to the touch. Drift lay down on the green carpet and nodded his head.

'I like it,' he said. 'You've done well.'

Daisy bobbed his head and came round and sat beside his friend.

'You'll be all right in the morning,' soothed the badger. 'I'm sure of it.'

Drift nodded his agreement. 'It was a close thing, though.'

'It was,' agreed Daisy, 'too darn close.'

They settled down to doze in their new home away from the wind, safe from the humanthings and their wicked inventions.

But they were not to remain undisturbed for long.

'Someone's coming,' whispered Drift urgently, raising his head, his ears and nose twitching and flexing and checking for scents and signals.

Daisy stood up and flexed his shoulder muscles ready to defend the entrance of their rotten-treed residence, for he imagined a pesky stoat might be in the vicinity. A stoat was never a match for a badger, not a badger of the wisdom and power and cunning of Daisy Willowpop. Daisy would show him who was the boss. Daisy would box him round the ears and send him packing.

'I think it's a dog!' warned Drift, but already it was too late for the stinky canine bundle of energy had pushed its way past Daisy, and was now busy inspecting everyone and everything inside the house.

''Ello,' it said, 'what are you two doing in here?'

It was a young spaniel and its tiny docked tail was bouncing about as if on a new spring.

'Everything all right then?' it continued, determined to stick its nose into everyone else's business. 'You look a bit miserable I must say,' as it sniffed Drift and Daisy in turn. 'What's been going on here then?' It couldn't or wouldn't stand still for a moment. 'Been in a bit of bother, have we?' Worse still it persisted in regularly laughing in that crazy way young spaniels have. 'Come on, come on, you can tell me. What have you two been up to?' it persisted, running up and down, and giggling, 'Arf,arf,arf!'

'We are resting, if you must know,' said Daisy. 'My friend has been hit. Shot in the leg.'

'Has he now? Terrible thing. Bit slow off the mark was he? Only got himself to blame, no doubt. You have to keep on your toes in this game, like me. Arf, arf, arf!'

'They shouldn't be shooting at deer and badgers,' said Daisy.

'You are right there, mate! Righter than you know. They should be shooting at the blinking pheasants. You haven't seen one round here have you? I have lost one, you see. I thought I could smell it, in here but I think it must be you.'

'We do not smell like feathered pheasants!' said Daisy indignantly.

'No, may be not, perhaps you don't, sorry about that. But there's a competition on, you see, and I so want to win it.'

'A competition?' asked Daisy, not really wanting to know the fine details.

'Aye lad, the span that collects the most pheasants gets to keep one, you see, and that is a prize worth having I can tell you.'

'What is your name?' asked Drift.

'Eh? Oh, they call me Pumpkin, no laughing now, Pumpkin, the humanthings call me, stupid I know, but my real name; my official spaniel name is Henry the fifth.'

'Well Henry five,' said Daisy, standing up and crossing his legs, 'there are no blessed pheasants in here, dead or alive, so do you mind awfully buzzing off and leaving us in peace. And be a good woofer and don't give away our position to anyone else.'

'All right mate, all right. Keep your hair on. It isn't my fault your friend got winged, you know. He'll be all right anyhow,' said

Pumpkin, dashing to Drift's rear to take one final look at the damage. 'Aye, he'll be all right that's for sure, I have seen a heck of a lot worse than that. Far worse.'

'Let's hope he will be,' said Daisy.

'See ya then,' said Pumpkin, as he dashed toward the doorway, pausing for one final look round at his newfound friends, before hurtling out and back into the woods.

'What a complete clown,' said Daisy.

'He didn't seem so bad, for a dog,' said Drift, settling down again.

'Spaniels are particularly stupid in my humble opinion. I don't know what they see in them,' said Daisy.

'Who sees what in who?' asked Drift.

'The dogs in the humanthings, and vice versa, that's what.'

'Oh that,' murmured Drift, yawning. 'They have lost their dignity, the dogs, sold their souls.'

'Aye, so you said,' said Daisy as he joined in the yawning competition and minutes later they were both fast asleep, curled up together and snoring, well away in the land of nod.

Eleven

The owl went off like an alarm clock at midnight. Hoot, hoot, hoot… scoot, scoot, scoot. Time to get up! Time to get up! The forest waits for no one!

Drift's eyes flickered open. It was pitch dark inside their tree house. Beside him Daisy was snoring like a dormouse in a coma. Moonbeams were playing around the entrance as clouds scudded across the face of the moon.

Drift stood up and gently tried his damaged foot on the moss. It wasn't right, but at least the numbness and pain had gone. He limped from the tree and stood bolt still outside the entrance. The owl had fallen silent and the only noise was the keen wind that whistled through the trees. Drift sniffed the air. It was a northerly, icy cold. He glanced up at a stand of silver birch trees. They were swaying this way and that and the few leaves that remained, shook violently as if keen to finally leave the mother tree.

He checked again for vital signs of strangers, sound, smell, sight, but there was nothing. A skein of night flying geese high above crossed the face of the moon, heading south for warmer climes. Drift was hungry again but before he could begin feeding two ponies trotted into the clearing. They were strangers. The first was black and white and the other dark brown. They were first year foals, still playful in that silly horsey way they have, and they were not much older than Drift.

'Watcha,' mumbled the brown one, spotting Drift, 'good feed here is it?'

'I don't know yet. I was just about to try it out.'

'Well don't hang about, young fella. See good feed; eat good feed, that's my motto, for if you don't, you can be sure some other fat and greedy beast will munch it all up before you.'

'That is very good advice,' said the other one, languidly, strolling over to where they stood. 'Only the other day we came across a clearing of luscious feed but before we could get a-chomping four fallow deer stags, four mark you, lowered their antlers and charged. Not to be messed with they weren't. We had to make a sharp exit, didn't we, Gordon? Nasty business it was. Very nasty.'

'Aye,' said the first one. 'You're not a fallow are you?'

'Nope,' said Drift. 'Red and proud of it.'

'Aye, thought you were. Feed away young friend, we will not bother you. We have no quarrel with the reds.'

'Any humanthings about?' asked Drift, taking his first nibble.

'Not now,' said Gordon. 'Awful palaver yesterday though. Firing pipes, dogs, the lot, you name it.'

'I know,' said Drift. 'We were caught in the middle of it. They shot my hoof!' And he waggled his damaged foot for their inspection.

'Goodness me, you were lucky there, and who's *we*, if you don't mind me asking,' said Gordon glancing back through the trees as if checking for strangers.

Right on cue Daisy stumbled from the entrance of the tree, yawning and scratching the top of his head, while rubbing sleep from his eyes.

'Drift, you rascal,' he said sleepily. 'Why didn't you tell me you were up and about? You should have woken me.'

'The badger's my good friend,' explained Drift. 'We are travelling together.'

'Oh aye. To where, exactly?' asked Gordon, never once pausing from ripping the grass from about their feet.

'The Black Woods,' said Drift, and as he said that, Daisy came scampering up beside them, nodding his acquaintance to the ponies.

'That's not so far now,' said Gordon, 'you should be there by morning, but watch yourselves. The Black Woods is a dangerous place.'

'How so?' asked Daisy.

'We know of creatures,' said the brown pony, glancing around again, 'that have entered the Black Woods and have never been seen again.'

'No!' said Drift, whistling through his bright teeth.

'Yes,' insisted Gordon, nodding his head, shaking his most attractive blond mane. 'Straight up, as sure as I am standing before you.'

'I don't believe in silly stories like that,' said Daisy. 'They are made up to frighten innocent creatures like us.'

'Think what you like, pal,' said the brown one, 'but we knows what we knows. Go in there at your peril, I am telling you.'

'He's right, you know,' said Gordon, and then, 'Oh well, cheerio, we must be off now,' and he kicked the ground hard for no apparent reason. 'I am dying for some water. We are going down to Hangman's Pool for a drink and a paddle. Sure you don't want to tag along?'

'Thanks, but no,' said Daisy. 'We have some important business up ahead.'

'In the Black Woods?' asked Gordon.

Daisy bobbed his head.

'Well you be careful now,' said the pony, and with that he whinnied stupidly and broke into a canter and hoofed it noisily away and onward into the cover of the trees, the brown fella racing behind crying out: 'Wait for me! Wait for me!'

Afterwards Drift said, 'What do you suppose they meant by that?'

'Old mare's tales,' said Daisy dismissively. 'I wish I had a fresh hamburger for every silly story I've been told in this forest, and especially, it has to be said, by the horses. They are never happy unless they are spreading rumours and scandal and gossip.'

'Don't mention that word if you don't mind,' scolded Drift.
'What word?'
Drift struggled to bring himself to say it.
'Ham…ham…hamburgers,' he finally managed to spit out.
'Oh that, sorry.'
After that they fed for an hour and then decided to move on again, leaving behind forever the safety and homeliness of their fallen tree home of which they had become quite fond.
'I have a feeling we might arrive there by dawn,' said Daisy, striding out ahead with renewed vigour.
'You mean to the Black Woods?'
'Yep. Course. Where else? It's where we are headed, isn't it?'
Drift bobbed his head. He knew well enough that was where they were going, though he did so with some trepidation. Would the reds be there? Would uncle Mo be there to welcome him? Would uncle Mo be nice and kind and be pleased to see him? And were there really fairies in the Black Woods, and what was the truth in the horsey stories of creatures vanishing? There was a lot to think about and not so much of it was good.

The icy wind increased and began howling words of warning. It blew the clouds clear across the country and the sun must have been particularly tired that day for it was very late getting up. But when it did, the watery rays shone across the forest like a beacon from heaven itself.
Drift and Daisy chose to rest after a long night's travelling. They were lying in the undergrowth at the top of a small hill. Before them for as far as they could see from left to right was open pasture, and beyond that, a winding river slithered across the meadows like a vast golden snake, the early morning sunlight glistening on the quivering water.
On the far side of the river as far as they could see was the Black Woods. They could understand now why it was named that way for the woodland was so dense, so impenetrable, so unwelcoming,

that little sunlight made it to the forest floor, even on the brightest of days. The thick forest was seemingly plastered to the ground like one gigantic black slug barring the way ahead, like some dangerous frontier that must never be crossed.

Drift shivered. 'The Black Woods?' he gulped.

'Yep, looks that way,' said Daisy. 'In there somewhere are your brethren. All we have to do now is find them.'

Drift tried hard to banish from his mind the negative thoughts that insisted on swirling through his young brain.

'It is a beautiful morning,' he eventually said, in an effort to remain upbeat.

'Glorious day,' agreed Daisy. 'Glorious! A glad to be alive day. Come on young fella. Today is the day when everything is decided.'

'Decided?'

'Yep. Today will decide your destiny, young Drift, my travelling buddy, extraordinaire. Today is the most important day of your young life. Come on. Follow me sunbeam, into the woods, into the trees. Into the trees!'

Drift watched the badger haul himself from the undergrowth and begin the long trek down the hill. There was something jaunty in his step that day.

'I'm coming,' yelled Drift after him. 'I'm coming. Don't you dare go without me,' yet with each passing step that took them one pace closer to that strange place, each beat of his quickening heart, he wondered what exactly lay in store for him, for them, and indeed whether he should ever enter that dark and hostile looking place at all.

Twelve

When they arrived at the river they found it was bigger and faster and colder and wider than they could have imagined, and worse than that, there was no bridge across.

'I'll have to follow the bank till we find a fallen tree,' said Daisy, 'I am not venturing into that.'

They glanced left and right and gazed as far as they could see, but there was no sign of any bridge or any helpful fallen trees either.

'I think we should cross here,' said Drift.

'No can do,' said Daisy defiantly. 'I am not risking it in that icy water. I know badgers are supposed to be good swimmers but I never liked swimming much. Sorry pal, we'll just have to follow the bank till we can find somewhere else to cross.'

'We can cross here,' insisted Drift, 'you can jump on my back.'

Daisy stared at the young fawn as if he were joking but the look on Drift's face told him different.

'You think you can carry me?'

'Don't see why not,' said Drift. 'Come on. Jump up, let's give it a go, just be careful where you place those sharp claws of yours.'

'All right, if you say so, but on your head be it,' said Daisy, and he leapt up on to Drift's back, almost falling off the other side as he struggled to gain his balance.

'Steady!' urged Drift.

'I am just getting settled,' said Daisy. 'Nicely balanced.'

'Ready then?' asked Drift.

'Ready as I will ever be.'

It was true, Daisy really wasn't that heavy and Drift could carry him easily enough, just so long as the badger sat perfectly still and didn't sink his claws into Drift's coat. The fawn limped toward the riverbank. They both took one last look left and right. The icy water was hurtling by, gurgling and spluttering as it swept along like some crazy vast wild animal rushing down from the mountains.

Drift set his front right foot into the water and eased it down on to the gravel bed beneath. He was relieved to find it was solid ground, not slippery mud or soft sand. In followed the second foot.

'It's cold,' said Drift, shivering, his eyes already beginning to water.

'Not up here,' said Daisy cheekily, gazing about him, suddenly quite enjoying his high and dry position.

A pair of blue jays above them in the oaks stopped nuzzling one another and stared down at the strange sight.

'Just look at that,' said the first.

'Doomed to disaster,' said the second.

'Fools of the highest order,' said the first.

'Jason, for once in your life, I agree with you, they must have a screw loose,' and they both began wittering and tittering.

Down below, in went the damaged foot. Again it landed on solid ground, which was a relief because if any hoof was going to give way, if they were to fall, it would surely be that one. One more careful pace forward. The water was deeper now and faster flowing. Daisy didn't like the look of it at all.

A shoal of bad tempered trout zipped past, one yelling out, 'Oi you! Mind where you are going, landlubbers! This is fish street don't you know! Whatever next.'

'Shut up scaly bum!' shouted Daisy. 'Ignore them, Drift.'

Drift wanted to giggle but managed not to. He was too busy maintaining his balance, taking the next step into still deeper water.

'My toes are getting wet!' moaned Daisy, trying hard to sit higher on Drift's shoulders.

'Lucky you,' said Drift, as the water level neared the height of his back.

They were in the centre of the river now where the current was at its most powerful. Drift began to lurch to the left, forced that way by the sweeping power of the current. Daisy feared the worst. The look on his face was one of terror. He hated swimming, he hated getting wet, he hated everything to do with water, and worse than that, his dreams often involved running from crazy dogs and plunging into swollen rivers to escape. Worse still, those same dreams often involved him drowning. A truly terrible death that is, drowning. He fell silent, not moving a muscle, holding on ever tighter; fearing the worst.

Drift was now leaning dangerously to one side, and even he was beginning to think the unthinkable. They were going to keel over and capsize. It would happen any moment now. Something deep inside Daisy's head told him to move to the right side and that little movement brought Drift back to the straight and narrow.

'Good move,' said Drift, breathlessly. 'Well done.'

'I thought so to,' said Daisy proudly, and with Drift's next step they were suddenly in shallower water.

'Nearly there!' encouraged Daisy.

Then they were out, standing on the far bank, Drift frantically shaking his body to rid himself of the icy water.

'Well done!' screamed Daisy, jumping down and dancing a crazy little badger dance on the freshly nipped grass. 'Well done I say.'

High above them the jays exchange a look, one of complete surprise, and in there somewhere was a tiny note of admiration.

Drift stood before the badger, panting. For a moment he couldn't speak at all and when he did he said, 'Guess what I want now?'

'No idea. What?'

'A drink of cold water,' and they both started laughing crazily as Drift returned to the bank and lowered his head and began drinking his fill.

'Didn't think we were going to make it there for a moment,' said Daisy, joining him.

'Neither did I,' agreed Drift, finishing his drink. 'Frightening, wasn't it.'

'You can say that again.'

'I was terrified.'

'Me too. Ready to press on?' asked Daisy.

Drift peered up at the gigantic trees before them. They really did appear to be totally black. How peculiar.

'Ready as I will ever be,' said Drift.

And with that Daisy began to sing. Drift had never heard him sing before and the funny thing was, he couldn't sing for rotten nettles, not a note.

Marching on together! Together we will go!
Marching on together! Searching for uncle Mo!
Marching on together! Together we will go!
Marching on together! Looking for uncle Mo!

Drift giggled inwardly for he didn't have the heart to tell his friend he couldn't sing at all. It was painful to the deer's ears. But other than that, the words were vaguely sensible, for Daisy that is, vaguely sensible.

Inside the forest the canopy was so dense that little light ever reached the ground. The forest floor was a mass of rotting oak and holly leaves and fir cones with the occasional sapling desperately trying to force itself upwards into the sunlight, striving for life. Because of the lack of light little grass grew there, and that accounted for the lack of herbivores living thereabouts, creatures like Drift. Daisy was fine, he could nose out a meal just about anywhere but Drift had to be careful, or he would go hungry.

There were animals in the dense forest of course and in some numbers too. They had both detected the strong scent of a healthy colony of local badgers, and that tickled Daisy pink for he wondered if they might be distant relatives, he pondered whether he should stop and say hello, but the badgers had all retired to bed and were fast asleep in the setts somewhere way below their busy feet.

In the treetops squirrels ran this way and that, squabbling crazily over the best acorns and chestnuts and fir cones as squirrels always do. Fox tracks were evident too, but they had also seemingly turned in, and that was no bad thing, for a bad tempered fox could be a real nuisance, and they were both thankful they neither saw nor heard a single one.

They travelled on for half a day without meeting a soul and without seeing anything decent that Drift could eat. Finally, in the middle of the day they came to a small clearing where the grass had flourished, but because of the shortage of feed, it had been mercilessly grazed.

'Not a lot there for you,' said a wise Daisy, staring down at the neatly trimmed sward.

'It'll be fine,' said Drift, 'with my smaller, sharper teeth I can feed after the big ones have fed.'

'The big ones have been here?' said Daisy.

'Oh yes,' said Drift, raising his head, grass falling from his mouth. 'The big ones have been here for sure.'

'Your big ones?' clarified Daisy. 'Reds, you mean?'

Drift sniffed the breeze.

'Oh yes, and not so long ago. I have spotted their business too, if you know what I mean. Open your eyes, Mister Badger, but I forget, your lot are all so darn short sighted.'

'Not that short sighted, we aren't!' said Daisy in a hurry, stumbling into stands of red deer poo. 'Oh yeah, I see what you mean.'

Drift laughed noisily through his nose and returned to his hectic feeding.

Half an hour later they moved on again and back into the semi darkness of the forest. All went quiet, and for some strange reason even the birds fell silent.

'The birds are quiet today,' said Drift.

'They are moulting,' said Daisy. 'Losing their feathers, preparing to grow new ones for the winter. You'd be quiet too if your coat suddenly fell out.'

'Yes, I suppose I would,' said Drift, imagining for a moment the hideous picture of the pair of them with no coats, naked in the forest, an object of laughter and ridicule for everyone else to see. What an awful thought, and how cold would that be, standing about with nothing on? It didn't bear thinking about.

'And no fairies here either,' grinned Drift.

'Course not!' said Daisy. 'Told you so. Old mare's tales. Total baloney, that's what it is. Absolute twaddle!'

They travelled on through the Black Woods for two more days and nights with nary a sign of red deer anywhere.

'This is hopeless,' said Drift, coming to a standstill. It was mid afternoon as they rested under a vast and naked sycamore tree. 'Perhaps that daft cuckoo-swallow was making at all up. He took your ring for nothing. May be I was mistaken earlier too.'

Daisy thought back to Bread n' Cheese and wondered where he was now. What a chump, thinking he was a swallow. It was as ridiculous as if he, being a fine badger as he was, thinking he was a donkey. Hee-haw! Hee-haw! How ridiculous. You are what you are, as Mother Nature intended, you can never change it, so there is no point in ever wishing you were something or someone else. He was just about to share those profound thoughts with Drift when a roar hurtled through the forest on the still wind.

'What on earth was that?' said Drift, getting to his feet and swivelling his antennae.

'I will tell you what it is!' said Daisy triumphantly. 'It's the roar of a stag! And unless I am very much mistaken, it is the roar of a red deer stag!'

'You think so?' said Drift excitedly, dancing up and down on the very end of his hooves.

Daisy nodded and said, 'Come on! Come on! Follow the sound. It could be your uncle Mo, and he's not so far away.'

Drift glanced at Daisy who was already striding up the incline in the direction of the bellowing that still came, persistent calls from an angry sounding animal, and a big brute at that. At the top of the bank the land flattened out and the trees were not so dense there. Walking between them became easier as more light filtered to the ground. A moment later they were aware of a barred wooden fence to their left and beyond the fence was open pasture that fell away down into a shallow valley. They crept to the fence and crouched down in the thick undergrowth.

'Look!' said Daisy triumphantly. 'Look at that! Red deer! Hundreds of 'em.'

Drift's eyes widened as he stared down on the moving mass of deerfolk below.

'I am so excited!' he said. 'I'm so excited! I've never seen anything like it!'

'Do you know what, Drift? Neither have I. Not so many in the one place at the same time.'

On the open ground between the fence and the foot of the valley a vast stag appeared as if from nowhere, strutting his stuff this way and that, waggling his impressive antlers at all comers as if he owned not only the entire herd, but the whole forest too. The beast roared again and every living thing, animal and plant, paid close attention.

'Do you think that could possibly be uncle Mo?' said Drift.

'It could be,' said Daisy, 'I don't see why not.'

For a moment the stag ignored the herd. It fell silent. It sniffed the wind. It looked nervous. It was staring beyond the boundaries of its immediate territory. A moment later it glared directly at Drift and Daisy. In the next second it was walking toward them, slowly at first, and never once averting its gaze, not rushing, but striding purposefully with intent toward the pair of them.

'I think it's seen us,' said Drift.

'Looks that way,' said Daisy, 'and it doesn't look happy.'

It was true, it didn't look happy at all, and now it was only twenty paces away.

'I wonder if we should make a discreet exit,' said Daisy, gawping at the needle sharp set of antlers that sat majestically on top of the stag's head, and then behind him for any potential getaway route.

'We can't do that!' said Drift. 'It's what we came for. We can't leave now,' and even as he said those words Drift was examining the stern adult face that was bearing down on them. 'I am sure it's uncle Mo, you know,' he said. 'Certain of it, and what a truly magnificent creature he is, don't you think, Daisy? We'll be all right now. You'll see.'

Thirteen

The stag came on until it was standing immediately before them. Daisy wriggled his body deeper into the cover of the bracken.

The huge beast stopped in front of them, its dark eyes unblinking.

'Show yourselves,' it said, in a deep voice that made the holly leaves tremble. 'I know you are in there. Show yourselves. I am not a fool.'

Drift stood up and tried vainly to smile.

'And the other creature too.'

Drift peered down at the badger.

'Stand up Daisy, he won't hurt you.'

Daisy nervously stood up and glanced into the stag's huge brown eyes, before averting his gaze. It was an unwritten rule of the forest that you never looked into the eyes of a superior beast until you were invited so to do.

'What is your name?' boomed the stag.

'They call me Drift, Mister Stag.'

'What is your business here? These are our lands.'

'He's a red deer fawn…' butted in Daisy, but before he could finish the stag interrupted.

'I can see that! Don't interrupt me. I am not an idiot!'

Drift spoke again. 'I have lost my herd.'

'That is particularly careless of you.'

'And Daisy here, the badger chap who is really a goodger, helped me to find you. The thing is, we are looking for my uncle Mo. You couldn't possibly be my uncle Mo, could you?'

'Certainly not! You know of the deer known as Mo?'

'Well yes, in a funny kind of way, though I have never met him, he is my mother's brother, my uncle so to speak.'

'And where is your mother?'

Drift couldn't bring himself to answer.

'Accident,' butted in Daisy, glancing away, 'on the highway.'

'Ah, that caper,' said the stag, 'humanthings I suppose?'

Daisy nodded. Drift looked sad.

'Unfortunately you have arrived here too late. Your uncle Mo, as you call it, is no longer with us.'

Drift gulped. He always knew the Black Woods was a dreadful place and there was no good news to be found here.

'I am Big Richey,' said the Stag, throwing his head up to better display his magnificent headgear, just in case the interlopers hadn't yet spotted it. 'I am the big chief of all the red deer residing in the Black Woods and the Farley Enclosure. I hope that is clear to you. You can call me, Chief.'

'We are very pleased to meet you, Chief,' said Daisy, 'but the thing is, we were wondering if young Drift here could join the herd. Seeing as he is one of yours and has none of his own kind to run and play with. It would be very fine of you if you would accept him into your great family. Very mag… mag… magnan…magnanipous of you.'

Drift tittered.

The stag peered down at the stupid badger through the bottom of his eyes. The creature could barely speak properly, though he had at least taken the trouble to attempt to return the foundling, and not many others would have done that.

'I might be so inclined,' said Big Richey, peering again at Drift. 'So long as you come on my terms.'

'And what are your terms?' asked Daisy, keen to see his friend all right.

'*It* will start at the bottom.'

'I am not afraid of starting at the bottom and working my way up,' said Drift.

'The fawn will eat only when his seniors have eaten, *it* will always run at the rear of the herd, *it* will keep its thoughts to itself, *it* will always obey me in all things, unquestioningly, and finally, *it* will *never* mention the name of Mo ever again. Is that understood?'

'I can do that,' said Drift, though Daisy could hear the reluctance in his voice.

'I will tell you what I will do,' said Big Richey. 'You can go away and sleep on my thoughts. Tomorrow you may return to the herd. We shall be breaking camp and moving out an hour before sundown. If you are here at that moment then I shall know you are prepared to accept my wishes. But if you are absent, I shall know that you are not. In that case you shall be an outcast forever. Make no mistake about it; this is your one and only chance, Drift. You will never be invited to join the herd again. Is that clear?'

Drift cleared his throat and bobbed his head.

'Speak fool, don't nod!'

'Yes, Big Richey, er… I mean, Chief, I understand.'

'And another thing.'

'Yes, Chief?'

'Don't bring scruffy ears back with you tomorrow. All badgers are bad. Didn't your mother at least teach you that much?'

'Oh, but Daisy is not bad, he's a fine friend, a true goodger.'

'There is nothing more to be said on the matter. Obey me!' and with that the self-styled king of the forest slowly turned about, shoved his nose into the air, and walked contemptuously away, back toward the herd, his herd, who were all watching his every move.

Daisy and Drift watched him leave and shared a look.

'Come on,' said Daisy, trying to sound cheerful. 'We have a whole day and night to play and feed and chat and make our plans.'

They turned about and hurried away from the valley and travelled through gently wooded countryside to where the feeding was better.

'Everything will turn out for the best,' said Daisy, 'in the end it will, you'll see,' yet it still all came out so unconvincing.

'Can't say as I liked Big Richey much,' moped Drift, already munching on tired dandelions.

Daisy thought he was an arrogant so and so, and he had another ruder word for him too, but wouldn't use it, not in front of Drift, not there and then. Big Richey, or whatever his real name was, was just the kind of beast that gave all the forest creatures a bad name, though he wouldn't say. Instead he heard himself saying: 'I suppose he has to be like that, to keep such a grand herd all together.'

'He was quite rude to you too,' muttered Drift.

'I have heard much worse in my time. I thought he was ruder to you, referring to you as *it*, indeed. What a blinking cheek!'

'Did he?' said Drift, 'can't say as I noticed,' but of course he had.

They fed for two hours more and slept for two, then played a happy game of tag and bite yer tail and then slept some more as the moon swayed its way across the sky, humming as it went. The owls returned and hooted and hooted and the foxes barked as Drift and Daisy curled up together and snored the remainder of the night away, safe and warm with just their happy dreams for company.

The watery sunshine woke them, playing across their faces like reeds in a gentle wind, that, and a solitary dragonfly that arrogantly perched on the far end of Daisy's snout.

'Pufft!'

Daisy blew air down his nose and the dragonfly skipped into the sky muttering: 'All right! All right! No need to get uppity,' before flying off in the direction of Hangman's Pool.

'I am hungry again,' said Drift.

'You are always hungry. That is only natural when you are growing like you are. Then feed,' said Daisy. 'You'll need to get as much food down you as possible. The herd is moving out today and you don't know how far and how fast they will travel. You will need to be well prepared. It could be an arduous trip.'

'What does arduous mean?'

'Something tough, like a hard and difficult journey. To begin with, you might find it quite wearing.'

That didn't bother Drift at all. He possessed a grand set of four legs and his damaged hoof was already healing well. He was a competent runner, better than competent some might say, and he knew it too. In a strange way he was looking forward to the test, if only it wasn't for the presence of Big Richey.

'I will miss you so much,' said Drift, settling to feed again. 'You are so clever.'

'I will miss you too, but you can always come back and see us at the sett. I am sure the herd will wander that way at least once through the year. You must come and see us all. Bring your new friends too. You will always be most welcome, you know that, don't you, Drift. In the end everything will turn out for the best. You'll see.'

'You have been the best friend I have ever had.'

'You will make many new friends. You saw how many youngsters there were gallivanting about. Before you know it you will be running with your brethren. You will soon forget all about me.'

'I shall never forget you, Daisy, never.'

After another feeding session Daisy yawned and that sparked Drift into yawning too.

'A short nap I think is in order,' mumbled Daisy, 'yes, shall we? One last nap before you begin your great trek.'

'Will you be all right returning by yourself?'

'Oh yes, don't you worry about me. I know the way home.'

'You will be careful at Blue China Farm, won't you, where the crazy dogs are, and that weird humanthing that can actually speak.'

Daisy giggled. 'Wasn't that funny? I almost broke down when it began speaking. I nearly had an accident in public. I would never have believed it if I hadn't heard it with my own ears.'

'Your scruffy ears,' teased Drift.

Daisy smiled and ran his claws over his ears.

'There's nowt wrong with my lugholes. Other badgers have commented on my ears most favourably, if you must know.'

'I'll bet they have.'

They shared another giggle and settled down to sleep in the thick and browning vegetation, a safe place where there was a good view out across a small nipped meadow, and shortly afterwards in the early afternoon, the forest reverberated to the sound of contented snoozing.

They hadn't been asleep for long when Drift woke first, as he was prone to do, conscious that his time with Daisy was rapidly slipping away. He glanced up at the sun. It seemed to be racing across the sky. In the next moment Daisy was awake too.

'Why is it,' said Drift, 'that when you want time to hurry up, the sun barely moves, yet when you want time to stand still, the sun gallops across the heavens as if being chased by the hounds of hell?'

'I don't know,' said Daisy. 'It always works out like that. I guess it is just the way of the world. It is something you have to learn to live with. We can't change it.'

Drift placed his chin on his knees; his hooves neatly tucked in beneath him, and closed his eyes.

A few minutes later Daisy said, 'Hey up, who is this then?'

'Who's what?' said Drift, slightly bored this time, his eyes still tight shut.

'This!' said Daisy, greater excitement clear in his voice.

Drift opened his eyes and peered out across the meadow. At first he didn't quite believe what he saw and closed and opened his eyes again in case he was dreaming. But it was no dream. Before them standing on the field, smiling directly at them; was a comical looking stag. Its left antler was completely missing and to compensate for the weight on the other side of its head, it held its face at an odd angle that suggested it was always about to ask a question.

Drift jumped up and took a pace forward. The lopsided stag took a pace forward too and then it smiled and said: 'You're Drift, aren't you?'

Drift beamed and took another pace.

'How on earth did you know?'

'You are the image of your mother.'

'Are you my uncle Mo?'

'I most certainly am.'

'Daisy! Daisy! Come out and meet my uncle Mo!'

Daisy stood from the bracken and sauntered over toward the one antlered stag.

'We are so pleased to meet you,' said Daisy, 'very pleased indeed.'

'Uncle Mo,' said Drift, 'Daisy brought me here, all the way across the forest. I should never have made it without him.'

'I am most grateful to you,' said uncle Mo. 'I shall forever be in your debt. Now come along, I think you had better tell me all about it, don't you.'

Fourteen

They paused under a cavernous oak tree as Drift began telling uncle Mo of everything that had happened to them.

'And that's when we met Big Richey.'

Mo smiled benignly.

'There is nothing *big* about him,' yawned Mo. 'I call him Tricky Ricky.'

'He said you were no longer with us,' said Drift breathlessly. 'We thought you were, well, dead, didn't we, Daisy?'

The badger nodded; keen to speed up the conversation, for he was eager to make a start back to the sett before it grew dark.

'So what happened between you and Big Richey?' asked Drift. 'Did he defeat you on the field?'

Mo thought about that one for a moment and chose his words with great care.

'In a manner of speaking he did, but not as you might expect.'

'Then how, uncle Mo? Please tell us more.'

'You are right. We had a fight, and the future of the entire herd rested on the outcome, for there was no other stag who would dare challenge Ricky or I. He is a big and powerful creature, it is true, but he is not the cleverest deer that ever roamed the fields. The simple truth is that I always had his match. He would push up against me, but I could hold him comfortably enough without exhausting my energy. He imagined we were well matched, but I possessed reserves he could only dream about. I knew that I would triumph in the end, I couldn't lose, not to him, it was my destiny you see, to defeat him just as my father had foretold so many moons before. I was to become the king stag and overall ruler of the forest.'

'So what happened?' asked Drift. 'Is it to do with your missing antler?'

Mo bobbed his head, in a sad way, Daisy thought.

'We were fighting on the rocky slopes over by Garrett's Wood. We had been tussling for more than three hours and truth be told, we were both becoming tired. He put in one tremendous last push that caught me a little unawares, but nonetheless I stopped him in his tracks. Fact is, I stopped him for good, and for the first time I saw something strange set deep within his eyes.'

'What uncle Mo? What?'

'Defeat, Drift, that's what I saw. A picture of total defeat reflected back at me. And what is more, I knew that he knew I had had seen it. He knew that I had his measure. He knew that he had lost.'

'And then?' asked Daisy.

'He turned and ran, or at least he started to.'

'And then?' persisted Drift.

'The rocks began moving.'

'The rocks began moving?' repeated Drift, incredulously.

Mo nodded wearily.

'A landslide?' asked Daisy.

Mo bobbed his head. 'It is still hard to believe it now, but that is what happened. Large flat boulders began slipping down the slope, taking me with them. I glanced up and Tricky had stopped and turned about. He must have heard the rumbling and roaring as the ground slipped away in front of us. At the foot of the slope the boulders came to a crashing standstill, as did I, and all seemed well enough, when one last long slab of cold, grey rock whipped down, flying through the air. I ducked, but too late. The rock took my antler clean away as it passed above my head. I heard Tricky snort in triumph. He saw his chance and bounded down the slope. Unmerciful he was; I guess I would have done the same, but even with one antler I was able to give him a fight, but not win. I could hold him, but I could no longer beat him. He drove me from the field, roaring and bellowing as if he had defeated me fair and square, when nothing could have been further from the truth, and when I glanced back he was standing proud, gloating, spittle dribbling from his bottom lip. I shall remember that image until my dying day.'

'Don't worry, uncle Mo,' said Drift, 'I'd rather stay with you anyway. We neither of us liked Big Richey much, did we, Daisy?'

'Certainly not!' said the badger, kicking the ground. 'Rude and arrogant he was. Didn't care for the creature at all.'

'I know what we'll do,' said Drift. 'Why don't we just ignore Big Richey and his crowd? Why don't we clear off and build a brand new herd all of our own?'

Daisy giggled.

Drift looked perplexed.

'I think there's something else you might need to achieve that,' said the badger, winking at Mo.

'Like what!'

'Like females, you know, like your mother,' said Daisy, grinning and smirking from ear to ear.

'Oh yes,' said Drift, 'I suppose so, I hadn't thought of that.'

'You don't need to worry about all that,' said uncle Mo, a mischievous look displayed on his lopsided face. 'Before the fight I took the precaution of cutting out ten of the best hinds, just in case something went awry. Tricky is so stupid he didn't even notice they were missing. We are all living peacefully over at Gill's Copse. I was on my way back there when I came across you two fast asleep in the bracken. And I'll tell you another thing, those hinds will sure as heck make a big fuss over you, young Drift, when they see you that is; you see if they don't.'

'You think so?'

'I am sure of it!'

'Well that's sorted that out,' interrupted Daisy, glancing at the scarlet sky. 'And if it's all settled and if you don't mind, I really must be off now. I'd like to make a start back while there is still some daylight for there is a fair way to travel.'

Drift glanced across at the badger, and the knowledge that this might be the last time he would ever see Daisy was clear in his mind.

'I will miss you so much,' he said.

'I will miss you too. Perhaps you could come over and see us one day. You will bring Drift over to see us, won't you uncle Mo?'

'I shall do my very best, Mister Goodger, you can rely on that.'

Daisy nodded and patted Drift's shoulder, firm but playful.

'Well,' said the badger, 'I told you everything would turn out all right in the end.'

'You did that, Daisy, several times, and not for the first time you were absolutely right.'

The badger nodded one last time at Mo and at Drift in turn and then with a heavy heart turned and ambled slowly away toward the trees.

'Goodbye!' shrieked Drift after his best friend. 'Goodbye, Daisy Willowpop! You glorious goodger, you! My very best friend.'

Daisy raised his front paw and waved back over his shoulder, but he didn't dare turn round for he didn't want his friends to see the tears that were tumbling down his face.

After he'd gone Mo glanced down at Drift. There were tears there too, but Mo was clever enough not to draw attention to them.

'Come on,' he said, 'let's make for Gill's Copse. There are ten fine creatures I am dying for you to meet.'

'And you think they'll like me?'

'Bound to, Drift, course they will. How could they not?'

They began cantering, something they both hugely enjoyed, chatting on the hoof, working up a sweat, kicking their legs high as they went.

'You have a limp?' said Mo.

Drift told his uncle all about the narrow shave with the humanthings and their deadly firing pipes. 'It's well on the mend now though. See, I can run beside you without any difficulty.'

Drift glanced up at his uncle and saw that he was smiling down. Then Drift said, 'So can we really start our own herd?'

'We can make a start, in time we can, but I haven't accepted the loss of the big herd yet. Not for anything.'

'How do you mean?'

'Tricky may have won a battle, aided by the mysterious flying stones, but he most certainly did not win the war.'

'How do you mean? What are you going to do?'

Mo came to standstill beside a small pond where the water was clear and cold. He bent down and began drinking and afterwards said, 'I am going to rest up for a year. I am going to look after myself, eat well, sleep well, get myself fit and strong, take lots of exercise, grow myself a fine new set of antlers, antlers the like of which have never been seen before, and when the time is right, when I am at my peak, and when Tricky will be at his laziest, I shall stroll on to the field and lay down my challenge. I shall roar a roar the likes of which the forest has never heard before. Big Richey, or whatever he likes to call himself, is in for the fright of his life.'

It all sounded so exciting to Drift. He couldn't wait for the year to fly by for he was desperate to witness the showdown that would decide the eventual future of all the reds in that part of the forest. Then he said, a touch of concern in his voice, 'And you'll win, uncle Mo, you will win, won't you?'

Mo was drinking again and as he raised his wonky head, water dribbled from his mouth and splashed down to the surface, making a magical tinkling sound as it fell.

'What do you think nephew?'

'Oh I think you'll win, I think you can beat him, uncle Mo, with two good antlers you definitely will. I am sure of it.'

'My thoughts entirely. I shall beat him fair and square. I shall drive him from the field and claim my birthright, and one day far in the future, little one, many seasons from now, you shall succeed me.'

'Really?' said Drift, his mind suddenly ablaze with thoughts of glories to come and victories on the field.

'Really!' confirmed Mo. 'For sure! That is how it will be. Now come on, we still have a fair way to go.'

Fifteen

When they arrived back at Gill's Copse the hinds greeted them just as uncle Mo had promised. They seemed genuinely pleased their leader had returned, and much more than that, they were tickled pink and intrigued with the cute fawn that uncle Mo, as he was known to all, had brought back with him. They all pushed in and surrounded Drift, taking it in turns to nuzzle up to the little creature with the handsome face and vibrant eyes.

Drift had never received attention and affection like it before, and though the sensation of suddenly being surrounded by creatures of his own kind was unnerving, it was also terribly exciting, an excitement he didn't fully understand.

Within minutes he had been accepted by everyone and during the day and night that followed, Drift would make great friendships that would last until the end of his days.

In the morning uncle Mo suggested they went on a trek, just the two of them.

'It is always a good idea to leave the hinds to themselves now and again. It keeps them on their toes, it keeps them guessing as to where we are and what we are up to. Understand?'

Drift wasn't sure that he did fully understand, though he was clever enough to realise that uncle Mo was imparting vital stag deerlore, knowledge that his mother could never have handed down. That morning, and forever after, he would pay great attention to everything his uncle said. Drift nodded, not wanting to appear stupid, and his uncle seemed happy enough with that.

In the middle of the morning they stopped at a large clearing where the ground was flat and the grass had been almost grazed out by hungry horses, judging by what little feeding remained.

Mo ambled to one side of the clearing and began nuzzling about in the tufted stuff. He appeared to be looking for something and a few minutes later he must have found what it was, for he called Drift over.

'Hey! Come and see! Look at these?' he said, struggling to keep his lopsided head on the straight and narrow.

Drift ran over and glared down and grimaced.

'Toadstools!' he yelled. 'My mother always told me there were two things you must never eat, ragwort and toadstools!'

It was easy to leave the toadstools alone for they smelt horrid, but the ragwort was a different thing altogether, with their pretty yellow flowers and occasional sweet smell that seemed kind of inviting to the hungry herbivore. Occasionally they watched horses nibbling on the ragwort, though it would not be long before they fell terribly ill. Ragwort was bad, evil even, most of the creatures understood that, but toadstools were even worse. Toadstools were …were…the devil's work.

'Your mother was almost right,' said Mo. 'Most toadstools are indeed very bad, deadly poisonous some of them, which is why even ratty won't touch them. But some of them are not poisonous at all. Take these fellows for example. They are quite different from their brethren for they are not toadstools at all, but mushrooms.'

'Mushrooms?' said Drift. He had never heard the word before, *mushrooms*, and a funny word it was too. 'They all look the same to me,' he said, a frown fixed on his face.

'True, they may look the same, but these ones are special.'

'Special? How?'

'These ones, my little nephew, are magic mushrooms.'

Drift giggled and booted the ground.

The thought that a foul smelling toadstool could ever be described as magical was far-fetched in the extreme, even for his faintly scatty uncle Mo, who Drift had quickly learnt had some mighty funny ways about him.

'I tell you, these are magic mushrooms, and that is why I am going to eat them.'

'But you can't,' said Drift. 'You mustn't!'

Too late.

Uncle Mo had bitten off a mouthful and was busy chewing hard, smiling down as his jaws revolved, and worse than that, he was already searching for the next portion to follow.

'You try some,' he mumbled, through a full mouth.

'No thanks. Not in a million years! I am not eating them,' said Drift, turning away and glancing back across the deserted clearing.

'Look! If they were deadly poisonous I would have fallen ill by now, wouldn't I,' said Mo, grabbing a third portion. 'I tell you; these ones are fantastic. Try a few to please your old uncle Mo. You won't regret it.'

Against his better judgement Drift bent and sniffed the things. Were they plants or animals? It was difficult to tell. They didn't look like a plant, and they sure didn't smell like a plant either.

'Go on then,' urged Mo. 'Try one, you might like it.'

Drift nipped off two small ones and began chewing. They were not as bad as he expected. Reasonably sweet as it turned out, though he would never eat them in future out of choice, if there were sweeter plants to feed on, but he had to admit, if he was really really hungry, and there wasn't anything else to eat, he just might try them again. It was true; they were not so bad after all, quite nice for a change, in fact they were strangely moreish.

When Drift glanced up, the sky had turned purple.

He glared at the sky as if it was playing tricks on him, and then back at uncle Mo. Unless Drift's eyes were deceiving him, his uncle's eyes had swollen to twice their normal size, and there, set upon his wonky face, his one antler almost sticking straight up, was a most peculiar expression. Queerer still, uncle Mo had turned bright yellow, and orange, and green. Yellow, orange and green!

Drift shook his head and closed his eyes tight shut and opened them again. Uncle Mo grinned back like a contented pig, and in the next moment he began chuckling and giggling like the little humanthing had, and after that he began trotting around the clearing, kicking up his legs, humming a most peculiar tune as he went.

Against his better judgement Drift fell in behind, he couldn't help himself, and then began strolling, or was it dancing, around the clearing in ever decreasing circles that would eventually make him terribly dizzy. To make matters worse uncle Mo was now singing a silly song as they went.

On the third circle Drift became aware that other creatures had joined in the dancing. Strange creatures too, while yet smaller ones had flitted in from around the edge of the clearing, yelling and screaming and gurgling in merriment. Drift had never seen anything like it before. His eyes hurt as he struggled to focus on the newcomers.

He thought they were green and purple and yellow and orange, and they didn't appear to be running on the ground, but flying just above the surface of the turf. Drift shook his head and stared once more. They had wings! The creatures boasted wings, like a dragonfly's. They must be fairies, he thought, and that was the last thing he remembered about anything before he lay down and tumbled into a deep sleep, a kind of heavy all-consuming sleep that he had never experienced before.

When he awoke it was daylight and it was raining. Everything looked grey. Perhaps it was the pitter-patter of the rain on his coat that had woken him. He was lying in the centre of the clearing and a few feet away was his uncle, sound asleep and snoring heavily, loud enough to keep strangers at bay. The snore was so loud that Drift would later swear that the evergreen fir trees close by shivered in time with each breath expelled.

Drift and Badger and the Search for Uncle Mo

Drift tried to stand up. It was then that it hit him. A headache the like of which he had never experienced before and one that he never wished to have again. It was as if the green woodpecker was inside his head, hammering to escape. He felt nauseas too, and when he eventually stood up, his legs shook violently, as if he had a fever. What the heck was the matter with him? Could it be that a terrible cold had landed upon him as he slept in the rain? His throat was dry and sore as if he had been scoffing on old gorse bushes and he was desperate for a cool drink.

'Uncle Mo,' he muttered feebly. 'Uncle Mo...'

The stag didn't move a muscle and wouldn't wake for several hours. Drift tried to make sense of it. He had eaten toadstools; he remembered that much, against his better judgement it had to be said, or mushrooms, as Mo had fancifully called them. It had always been against his wishes, but he had let himself be persuaded. They must have been poisonous after all, just as Drift had suspected all along, or why else would he feel so desperately ill?

Then Drift remembered the fairies dancing about him, giggling and shrieking. He glanced around the edges of the clearing. There was nothing to be seen, no fairies there, except a small hedgehog rushing about its business before it fell asleep for the entire winter.

Drift recalled the humanthing telling them of the fairies in the Black Woods, though they were not in the Black Woods any more, as he struggled to make sense of what he had seen, or thought he had seen.

He stood quite still in the rain, thinking hard, when a comforting sound floated across the clearing. It was a burbling, a gurgling; the sound of sweet water on the move, chuckling. Water in a hurry is always tastier than standing still pools. There had to be a brook close by, and with the rainfall the water level had risen and the burbling had grown louder. He staggered toward the stream and was grateful to thrust his entire head deep in to the cold water, shaking it this way and that as he did so. He drank his fill and soothed his throat as the icy water cleared his head, and afterwards he made his way back to the stag who was still snoring loudly.

Drift sniffed the grass close by and began feeding. He would *never* eat toadstools again, or mushrooms either, not in his entire life. It made common sense. Never eat anything when you don't know what it is, and what it might do to you. It was the age old advice that his mother had left with him, just as her mother before that, and it was as good now as it was when it was first issued by the Great Stag in the sky, when it was first ordained and handed down all those eons ago, before the earth was covered in trees, before the humanthings even existed, before anyone knew anything about anything. Toadstools spell great danger, everyone knows that, and you ignore the wisdom at your peril.

Never again. Never again.

Never. Never. Never.

Sixteen

It was two hours after that before uncle Mo finally woke up. He groaned and staggered to his feet and yawned, his vast tongue vibrating around his wide-open mouth before lolling over the side of his teeth.

'My throat,' he groaned, 'dry as a wasp's nest.'

Drift widened his eyes and stared at his elder. Mo's tongue was a peculiar shade of blue.

'How are you, anyway?' asked Mo.

'I'm fine now; thank you. There is sweet water over there,' said Drift, nodding toward the brook.

'Righty-ho,' said Mo, sheepishly thought Drift, as Mo turned and wandered unsteadily toward the stream that he could now hear through his aching head. Drift followed too for there was something he wanted to say, though he knew he would have to choose his words carefully.

Mo was guzzling water as if he hadn't had a drink for a week and before Drift could say anything else, Mo said: 'All right, all right. What's on your mind, little 'un? Something is, I can tell.'

'If you want to beat Big Richey...'

'There is no *if* about it!'

Drift tried again.

'If you want to beat Big Richey you will have to look after yourself better than this.'

'I know that!'

'I don't think you should eat mushrooms again until you are crowned king of the herd, or better still, never touch them ever again, I mean never.'

Mo raised his head, the water dribbling from his hairy muzzle as it plopped into the brook. He pulled a peculiar face as if thinking of faraway things and then he said, 'All right. I think you might be right. I shall *not* eat mushrooms again until I am crowned the king stag. Agreed?'

Drift grinned and bobbed his head. 'Agreed, uncle Mo. Agreed.'

One year rolled by in a blur of happiness as Drift ran and fed and grew with the hinds. Each morning at sunup he would accompany Mo on a long run through the forest, always following the same route, in a giant circle around their preferred feeding grounds. Drift was growing fast, but more importantly than that, Mo was visibly toning up his muscles.

In the evening Mo would trek out alone on another circuit, faster this time, more demanding, venturing further afield, and Drift was glad to see him coming back breathless and tired.

Mo duly lost the single antler and soon learnt to hold his head straight again, something that made him appear so much wiser and strangely, tougher too. It wasn't long after that when the new antlers began to show, something that fascinated Drift, and his first duty every morning was to inspect them and give Mo a detailed commentary on how they were progressing.

Both antlers were covered in protective velvet as they grew, and when the growing season was done, Mo would thrash his head in the gorse bushes to rid himself of the annoying covering. Drift stood faithfully by, inspecting and directing where yet more thrashing was required.

When it was finally done Mo stood proudly in the sunshine, his head held high, his eyes ablaze, for he could feel the fighting tools above him, and he knew they had become something special.

'Well?' he said expectantly, posing and glancing at Drift. 'Well?'

'They are truly magnificent, uncle Mo.'

'Each point is called a tine, Drift, so how many tines do I have? How many, little 'un? How many?'

Drift began circling the Stag, carefully counting as he went. One, two, three, four…

Mo was becoming mighty impatient.

'For goodness sake, Drift, how buzzard many?'

'Ten!' said Drift finally, still examining and recounting just in case he had made an error. 'Ten, uncle Mo.'

From the look on his face it was clear that Mo was disappointed at the news, and his shoulders slumped alarmingly.

'You thought there would be more?' murmured Drift.

Mo nodded. 'I did as it happens. Ten is less than a year ago. Big Richey will surely produce a head with more than ten. It will make it all the more difficult to defeat him. Can't be helped I suppose. I shall just have to take him on head to head with my ten.'

'But you don't understand,' babbled Drift. 'You don't understand at all. You have ten… on either side.'

Mo's mouth fell open. For a moment he was speechless.

'Ten on either side,' he repeated slowly, his face now a picture.

Drift grinned and nodded, his bright eyes reflecting the sunshine and the joy he felt in his heart.

'Ten on either side,' repeated Mo, as if he couldn't quite believe his good luck. 'But that is *more* than last year, a lot more. Twenty tines is a full head of antler and no mistake. I doubt if Tricky Dicky has ever had twenty tines in his entire life, surely not. Twenty tines, indeed! Who would have believed it? I wish my parents were here to see me now. Twenty tines, my word!' Mo shook his head this way and that, now fully aware of the frightening armament that protruded from the top of his head. 'Just how lucky am I?' he kept muttering, and as he did so he performed a crazy little dance. 'How lucky am I?'

'Perhaps it was all that exercise you did,' suggested Drift.

Mo nodded and waggled his headgear again, as if he had just discovered it for the first time. 'Perhaps you are right, Drift. I must remember that for next year. We will do exactly the same things next season. Exactly the same.'

'You must look after them.'

'Oh yes, you can be sure of that. The only things these beauties are made for, is putting Tricky Dicky in his place once and for all.'

Drift nodded contentedly for Mo now appeared truly formidable and it wasn't just the antlers, for the muscles on his chest and shoulders rippled like the barley in the fields at harvest time. Drift imagined there couldn't be a single creature in the entire forest that might stand up to his uncle Mo, and his twenty needle-sharp tines. Certainly not Tricky Dicky, nor even the bad tempered bull that made such a commotion every time it was spoken to over at Blue China Farm, no horse or donkey either, no other red or fallow deer, no single dog, nor even a pack of hounds, and certainly not any pathetic two legged humanthing, unless they were equipped with those frightening firing pipes of course, and even then Drift could imagine his uncle Mo sending them packing, screaming in terror as they fled from the very sight of him.

'So,' said Drift. 'When do we take him on?'

Mo noted the used of the word *we* when *he* would be doing all the fighting, but he let that pass for he knew that Drift's heart was in the right place. He meant well.

'There is no hurry, young Drift.'

'I thought you would want to get it done as soon as possible. Head down there and push him off the field.'

'You are a very clever creature in many ways, Drift, it is true, but on this matter, I have the accrued wisdom.'

'In what way?'

'We shall leave Tricky to an open field. He will, no doubt be challenged by all the young bucks. Each will heroically take their turn for it is written in their blood so to do, but none of them stand any chance of defeating him, for Tricky is too big and will be too well armed. We shall bide out time and hope the others wear him down a little. May be, just may be, he might become a little lazy. We shall let him become complacent.'

'What does that mean?'

'We shall let him believe that he has won, that he is once again the unchallenged king of the herd, we shall bide our time and lull him into a sense of false security, we shall leave it to the very last week of the rutting season, and then, and only then, when he least expects it, we shall stroll, nay, I shall stroll, on to the fighting grounds and lay down my challenge.'

Drift gazed up at his uncle in awe. He had never heard such talk before and finally he said: 'When will that be, uncle Mo? When?'

'Three weeks tonight, Drift. On the night of the full moon, everything shall be decided. Everything.'

Seventeen

And so it was that three weeks later on a cool afternoon they set out for the rutting fields, as a gentle breeze teased the forest, blowing silver dandelion parachutes like cobwebs through the trees, and across the brooks and streams.

Mo had kept to his word. He had not once eaten mushrooms since that crazy night with the fairies, and he felt all the better for it. His coat glistened, his muscles toned and pronounced beneath, while his twenty tines shone like gold above his head in the watery late afternoon sunshine.

It was one of those strange days when the sun and the moon were both in sky together, as if they had come out especially to witness the events to be played out in the forest far below.

Drift had woken early, when in truth he had barely been able to sleep at all. He could never remember being so excited. Today everything would be decided and Drift harboured no doubt that his uncle Mo would emerge victorious. It would serve Tricky Dicky right for being such an overbearing bully, for that was what he had become.

They had bade farewell to the hinds, each of them coming in turn to uncle Mo and Drift to kiss them and wish them well, and to remind them to take great care, for in the forest there are hidden dangers everywhere. Mo and Drift had departed to a chorus of concerned well-wishers and after that, they travelled through the forest with a sense of urgency in ever step, though not too quickly, for they were anxious to preserve every last ounce of energy for the trials to come.

Mo had warned Drift that the forthcoming tussle might continue through the night, and even in the morning there might not be a decision, but eventually he would win. Mo emphasised the point again and Drift believed him. Defeat was unthinkable.

When dawn breaks tomorrow, Drift thought, he was confident that his uncle Mo would be the undisputed king of the herd, the king of the forest, and Drift would be installed as his most important and trusted companion, related by blood. He would, in the space of one long day, become elevated to the leading family of the entire herd in the whole of the forest. It was almost unimaginable how things were about to change.

Two hours later Drift experienced a feeling of recognition creeping through his mind. This large oak, or was it that stubby holly tree, or maybe it was the way the silver birch trees were gathered together in groups, as if discussing the latest incredible news.

Have you heard? The red deer stag known as uncle Mo is on the warpath. He is about to challenge for the leadership of the entire herd, so they say.

Drift knew this part of the forest. He had been here before. He had been here with Daisy.

'I don't think we are so far away,' he whispered, anxious not to reveal their presence.

'You are right,' answered Mo. 'Tread carefully little one, move in silence, they will see us when I want them to see us, and not a moment sooner.'

There it was.

Exactly the same place where Drift and Daisy had lain in the undergrowth a year before, when they had peered down on the herd below. Not a lot had changed, except the herd had expanded still further in numbers. Lots of new blood was on display, scampering hither and thither, and most of it fathered by Tricky himself. That trend would have to be reversed.

Drift crept forward and lay on his haunches in the aging bracken. Mo remained in the shadows at the rear, the sun beginning to set at his back just as he liked it. Drift stared down. The herd appeared content. They sounded content too as they fed in peace and harmony, but where was the stag? Where was the king? There was no sign of him anywhere.

Drift checked again. He counted eight stags all told, but they were younger and frailer than uncle Mo, or even Tricky Dicky come to that. None of them could possibly be the king, the leader. So where was Tricky? Could something ill have befallen him? And if it had, who was in charge now? Who led the reds? For no herd can survive without a leader, without firm leadership, without management, without direction. In that case it would quickly fragment and dissipate across the entire county. Without a leader the herd was as good as finished.

For a second Drift imagined that Mo would simply have to stroll down the hill, make his presence known, roar a little, and take over the entire herd without a fight. Though he didn't like to say, that thought disappointed him. In truth it might be better for Mo, but Drift had been looking forward to the joust, the duel, between the two biggest and best stags in the forest for weeks and weeks. It was all he had been able to think about. Somehow it didn't seem quite right to simply walk on and takeover. Fait accompli. There had to be a display of might of some kind, or no one would ever take Mo seriously. It would lack authority, legitimacy, though Drift had never heard of such a word.

'Where is he?' whispered Mo, from the rear, through his deep voice as loud as he dare.

Drift glanced back over his shoulder. 'There is still no sign of him, uncle Mo. Nowhere. Perhaps he has been killed. Perhaps he has been hunted down by the humanthings and shot dead, or may be he has simply fallen ill and died, or perhaps he is sick and weak and sleeping somewhere in the reeds.'

Drift glanced back at the herd, all the way down the hill to the foot of the valley and across the river to the rising pastures beyond. The funny thing was there were one or two creatures there he thought he recognised. Young hinds from a year ago perhaps, though they were all bigger now of course, just as he was bigger himself. Drift was not yet fully grown, nowhere near, but much bigger and stronger than before.

Most of the herd were lying down, though a few still stood and fed in the last of the sunshine. Beyond the herd to the left was a bank of low juvenile oaks, but to the right, the bank of trees ended and Drift could see all the way across the river to where the ground climbed away in the distance. It played tricks on the eyes for it seemed so close, but the creatures there appeared tiny, proving the distance beyond doubt.

Drift searched again. He detected fresh movement. Not blind panic manoeuvres, nor a spooking sign, but something was happening for sure because the deer that had been lying down, all stood up and began gazing the same way, staring in the same direction, directly away from Drift. What was more, the creatures that had been feeding, ceased, and glanced up as if in respect, and at that moment Drift saw him.

A huge stag came strutting from behind the bank of oaks and began parading up and down on the far side of the river. He was in no hurry either and he clearly knew the others were all watching him. His head was held high, his powerful antlers gently swaying this way and that, as a timely reminder to any watcher stupid enough to dispute his right to lead, his right to everything. But was this stag Tricky Dicky?

Drift glanced back at Mo.

'I think he's here. It's a big stag anyway. I can't be sure.'

'I can see him Drift, I see him, though my eyes are not as sharp as your young eyes. Is it he, Drift? Is it him?'

Drift gawped back at the heavy creature. The stag was mighty impressive and for the first time Drift realised that this could be a fight to the finish. It would not be as easy as he had hoped. The opponent was huge and powerful and clearly well armed. Drift squinted and began counting the tines. He couldn't be certain but he thought he saw twenty, perhaps twenty-two. He considered telling Mo the news but thought better of it.

But was this Tricky that paraded before them? It didn't really matter for whoever it was; he would have to be defeated before uncle Mo could claim the herd as his own. Drift still couldn't be sure. They must get closer, though to do so might reveal their presence and that could be dangerous.

Mo began talking again, confident they could not be heard at the distance. 'He will have a good set of antlers no doubt, that is for sure, it is only to be expected.'

It was as if Mo had been reading Drift's mind.

Mo spoke again. 'Do not worry of that; just remember that I am stronger than he. I shall push him from the field. I shall dump him on his back in the river, and I shall do it before the entire herd to make absolutely certain that they all understand who is the new king. What do you say to that?'

'Yes, uncle Mo,' agreed Drift, 'I am sure you will,' but already he was glancing back toward the huge beast that had strolled a little closer. The creature appeared so big and strong, but worst than that, he looked mighty mean.

'When it starts,' said Mo, 'you are not to run on the fighting field. Understand?'

'Yes, uncle Mo,' replied Drift, unthinkingly, as youngsters sometimes do.

'It will be most dangerous. You could get killed.'

'I know, uncle Mo. I shall stay well clear.'

The river meandered across the foot of the valley like a giant silver snake. The stag ambled toward the water and began drinking. It glanced around at part of the herd that was on the far side of the river and then back to the others on the near side. The river was deep and wide and could be a real hazard to many creatures, but the majestic stag strolled across it as if it were the tiniest of brooks, as if it wasn't there.

Now it was on the same side at Drift and Mo, and coming ever closer. Two younger stags were feeding not far away. They stopped and glanced nervously at the leader. The big stag roared once and the two juveniles turned and fled. Satisfied with his work the king began parading nonchalantly up the hill.

'He's coming this way!' warned Drift.

'So I see,' said Mo. 'Don't panic. He is in for a big surprise.'

They watched him walk slowly toward them half way up the hill, almost directly at them. His back end was now facing the main body of the herd beyond, yet he knew they were all still watching him, and he was right. Drift stared across the breadth of the herd. Every creature respectfully watched. They might return to feeding nervously for a second or two, but they were still watching, still paying close attention to what the leader was about to do next. It was clear that someone was in for big trouble, and none of them wanted it to be them.

Three quarters of the way up the hill the stag did a lazy about turn and began ambling back down the slope, his large snout thrust into the air. He peered across his domain as if inspecting his subjects in turn. Drift paid close attention; anxious not to miss a single thing, his eyes glued, and he watched every member of the herd look away as the stag fixed his vision on each creature in turn.

'Phew,' said Drift. 'For a moment there I thought he'd seen us.'

'It is him?' asked Mo.

'Oh yes, no doubt about it now, though he's grown even more ugly in the year, don't you think?'

'He always was such an ugly beast,' sniffed Mo. 'Hideous! Face like a battered bat!'

Drift wanted to laugh aloud but didn't for fear of giving their position away.

'So what now?' asked Drift, but when he glanced back at uncle Mo he was surprised to see that his uncle was already on the move. In the next instant Mo had broken cover and was ambling down the hill, following Tricky Dicky almost in step, tracking him, twenty paces to the rear.

Drift's mouth fell open as he stared in silence.

Big Richey gazed ahead at the herd, quite unaware of Mo's presence. They were all intently watching, even more so than usual. He couldn't quite figure it out; they were peering up in perfect silence, not looking away when he fixed their eye lines as before. It was as if they were mesmerised. What was this all about? It almost seemed as though they were looking through him, indeed it appeared as if they looking behind him, as if they were staring at someone or something else. If they required another parade of authority then that was what they would get. He would stroll up and down the hill two or three times more until they showed him the appropriate respect.

Casually he turned about and showed his backside to the herd. He began ambling back up the hill. He raised his head and glanced forward.

Yeeks!!!!

What is that?

Facing him was another stag; and a big one too.

Wait a minute. Wait a minute. Big Richey recognised the beast. Surely it couldn't be that dreadful monster known as uncle Mo, the same interloper he had seen off and driven from the fields the previous season.

'You!' he said. 'You dare to return to my fields!'

'Hello Richey,' said uncle Mo, as relaxed as his could manage, and quite unable to keep that kindly grin from his face. 'Don't suppose you expected to see me here.'

'I am surprised you have the nerve.'

'Oh, I have the nerve all right. You see the herd belongs to me, and I have returned to claim my birthright.'

'Don't be so ridiculous! I drove you from the fields last year fair and square, and if need be, I shall do so again.'

'You drove me from the fields, that much is true, I will give you that, but fair and square it certainly was not.'

At that point Mo insolently turned about and began ambling up the hill, though not in retreat. It was a contemptuous gesture, displaying his backside to Big Richey, a move designed to annoy and tease him for he knew that it would work. He slowly ascended the hill and winked at Drift who had come out of the bracken and was standing on the brow, mesmerised just like all the others, watching the unmissable evening performance.

The sun was just about hanging on, spearing red shafts of sunlight horizontally across the forest, eager not to miss a thing, while the moon had moved even higher into the sky to gain a better view.

In line astern the stags came on toward Drift. When Mo was ten paces from him he turned about and faced his rival. Richey snorted, but he then turned about too, and began strolling back down the hill, unflustered, meaningfully, as if unconcerned, as everyone watched spellbound. Mo did not speed up but kept perfect step as they marched together back down the hill.

Big Richey slowed a little. Mo slowed too. Big Richey quickened. Mo quickened too. They were nearing the herd again, when Richey turned about and scowled and began heading toward his opponent. For a moment he considered throwing himself upon the interloper, but Mo was not yet ready to fight. The mind games could continue yet awhile. He turned about and started up the hill.

'Is that your nephew I see, standing on the brow?'

'It certainly is. His name is Drift and one day all this will be his.'

'Over my dead body! You had best warn him that he is in mortal danger. When I have finished with you, I shall deal with the runt on the hill.'

'Don't concern yourself with Drift. This is between you and me. Drift's day will come when you and I are riding through the skies.'

'Don't talk such nonsense!'

Drift watched them ambling up the hill, one behind the other. He saw they were talking to one another though he couldn't hear what they were saying. He thought he heard his name being mentioned, though he couldn't be sure. Why could they possibly be talking about him?

The notion struck him as to how alike the two stags were, like two giant bumble bees from the same hive, except Tricky was far uglier than his beloved uncle Mo. They were well matched though, that much was clear, similar in height and build and more importantly, they both boasted twenty tines apiece, fearsome fighting equipment that no creature in their right mind would ever confront, for any one of those tines could kill. Just the thought of it cooled Drift's blood. He wondered if he would ever find the courage to face down another creature such as these. The truth was, he thought probably not, and that unsettled him.

They were almost in front of him again. Mo winked once more, while Tricky stared at Drift unblinking, as if he was trying to convey some terrible message.

Mo turned about and this time everything was different. Big Richey stood his ground. He was not going to turn again. The promenading had come to an end. The fight was about to begin. Their eyes never left one another. There was no fear there on either side, simply determination to better the opponent, to be the victor, to be the king. Richey took two slow paces forward, and then abruptly broke into a sprint as if he had been shot in the hock by a humanthing's firing pipe.

Mo kicked off too, a little slow off the mark, thought Drift, but he had the lie of the land in his favour as he dashed down the slope and threw himself at Tricky.

For years afterwards the creatures of the forest that were fortunate enough to witness the event would tell their children and their grandchildren all about it, of the fearsome noise that crashed through the woodland as the two sets of antlers smashed into one another.

Every creature stopped still and paid close attention. The birds ceased singing, even the raucous magpies dashed to the highest boughs for a better view. The rabbits that had been frantically feeding away to the right all paused and took a few apprehensive paces closer, and stood on their haunches to watch the contest.

A local badger popped its head from its sett and reported back downstairs to the dozy ones beneath of the action in progress. Come along! Come along! You'll miss it! While two dog foxes, always at loggerheads, made their peace and stood together and commentated on the various moves and manoeuvres. A hare came running across the field and for one moment it seemed that it hadn't seen the joust in progress, when in reality it was simply desperate for a closer view. For now the hare would ignore the foxes; there was an amnesty on, all hostilities suspended.

Still the sun refused to set. This mighty argument was something too special to miss.

Sunset today will be delayed by ten minutes due to unforeseen circumstances.

The stags shook their heads violently to disengage but the complicated antlers stuck fast. Mo saw his chance and heaved his opponent backwards down the hill. The recent rain had made the slope slippery and Richey was struggling to hold his feet.

Mo pushed again and slid the beast down still further.

'You are bound to lose,' said Mo. 'I do not want to hurt you, Richey. Why don't you retire gracefully, leave the field in good condition, while you still can.'

'Over my dead body! You have the advantage of the slope here but the slope is evening out, and when it does, I shall push you back!'

It was true, the slope was evening out. They were right back down where the herd had been before. Some of the deer had scattered, eager to be out of harm's way, while others had crossed the river to the safety of the far side. Drift began down the hill too, anxious for a closer view.

The stags were fighting on level ground now, pushing and grunting and shaking their heads. Suddenly the antlers burst apart taking both of them by complete surprise. They each took three paces backwards before flinging themselves forward again with all their might, desperate to be the first to land a telling blow.

Crack!!!!

Their heads were locked fast again. Shaking, pushing, barging, cursing, twisting and thrusting. Richey changed tack and tried a sly donkey kick that caught Mo painfully on the right knee. It was a heavy blow and his leg was bleeding. Tricky smiled hideously believing he was gaining the upper hand.

'I can fight you all day and all night,' said Mo calmly. 'My stamina hasn't been tested, while you, you have been fighting all the young bucks for the past month.'

'Pufft!' answered Richey. 'The others were as nothing! They were simply good practice… for you. I am the one who is truly fighting fit and tried and tested. I am the one who is ready for anything. Who have you fought this year? That little runt up on the hill? He is about your level. You are slithering to defeat like a yellow bellied snake.'

The fight continued for another hour. Pushing, spitting, kicking, shaking, jabbing, verbal abuse, with neither stag willing to give an inch. Finally the sun grew tired and yawned madly and slipped away.

'I just can't stay up any longer,' it said, yawning again, and it went to bed with one parting remark. 'You must tell me all about it in the morning, Mister Moon, you promise me now?'

The moon winked its agreement across the star filled sky and returned to watching the contest.

The stags came apart again and this time they spilt left to right across the field. Mo ran hastily away and for an instant Richey imagined that he had seen him off; that he had won the day, but Mo was simply seeking a longer, faster, run up. He turned about and sprinted in toward Richey as if his very life depended on it, which in a way it did.

A thought flashed through Drift's head. This might be a decisive moment.

'Brace yourself uncle Mo,' Drift shouted. 'Brace yourself!'

In the fresh moonlight they closed on one another, leaping from the ground at the same moment, as they launched themselves through the air at their opponent.

Crack!!! Crash!!! Crack!!! Bang!!!

All those watching winced at the raw power generated, at the ferocity of the clash. No other creature in the forest could generate such raw power and terror, and no one could possibly withstand such a collision. Immediately Drift saw that this time everything was different. The stags pulled back slightly clear. Both were visibly shaken, dazed and staggering. Drift witnessed Richey's front legs shaking violently as if they were about to collapse beneath him, but it wasn't Richey he was watching now, but uncle Mo. Something was dreadfully wrong.

And then Drift saw a heinous sight, something so terrible that he would remember it for the rest of his days. He glanced away but quickly back as if to check.

Mo's left antler had sustained fatal damage at the base. It wavered and shook unnaturally in the wind and then tumbled forward, bouncing once on the end of his muzzle as it fell to the ground.

Richey shook his head. He was coming round, gradually recovering his senses. He glanced up and forced himself to focus on Mo, and saw the most beautiful of sights. His deadly foe, his only rival, his arch-enemy, his hated opponent, had lost half of his armament. It was splayed about on the muddy turf for all to see, just as it had been a year ago, broken and destroyed. Richey was winning. Mo was finished.

'Hah! Hah!' Richey shrieked. 'You are defeated! Beaten! You are a loser! Leave while you still can!'

The foxes shared a knowing look. The deer herd knew the game was almost over.

'I am not finished yet!' Mo snarled, 'I don't need two antlers to defeat you!'

But it was brave talk. In truth, Mo knew that he was in serious trouble. It was the same antler that had snapped the year before, precisely in the same place. Could it be that somehow the base hadn't fully healed? Could it be there was a weakness there? But there was no time to think of that now, for Richey had retreated thirty paces to turn about and charge again with maximum impact, intent on finishing the contest once and for all. Mo braced himself one last time. He set his remaining tines crossways to withstand the oncoming force, as Richey threw himself on his damaged opponent.

Crash!!! Crack!!!! Bang!!!!

Mo reacted cleverly and twisted this way and that to reduce the impact. He succeeded in stopping the razor sharp tines piercing his face, his eyes and neck, and he twisted again to force himself free. He had succeeded in stopping Richey in his tracks, but worse was to come for in the twisting, unnatural movement he had lost his footing. Mo had fallen to the ground. On the slippery turf he was struggling to regain his feet. He glanced up and saw Richey moving away, preparing for one final running charge. Mo must stand and face him or he was done for, but still he couldn't get up.

The hooves thudded closer.

'Your time is up!' screamed Richey, closing in. 'Prepare to meet the Great Stag in the sky!' as he thundered toward the side of Mo's prone body, twenty tines down and ready to strike. The moon winced at the sight of it all and it wasn't alone. The rabbits all looked away for they didn't wish to see, the hare too, though the magpies and foxes stared on with renewed interest. Could there possibly be a food bonanza for them before bedtime?

Drift had been edging ever closer. He had witnessed Richey's last charge. He had thought there was a meanness about it; and about

Richey too, a callousness that had no place on the duelling fields and no place in his beloved forest either.

Drift couldn't help himself. He galloped on to the field.

Mo detected his nephew from the corner of his eye as he braced himself for the inevitable heavy wound to the side.

'Back Drift! Back!' he shouted. 'What did I tell you?'

It was too late.

Drift only had eyes for Big Richey. The ugly stag had his head down and his antlers set as he hurtled towards Mo. This time Richey was determined to finish him off. As far as he was concerned the duel had gone on long enough, but in his eagerness he never once noticed the young one closing in from the side.

Drift rushed in, his heart beating like it had never beaten before. He felt the draught as the huge beast surged past him, those deadly tines homing in on uncle Mo's body. At the last moment Drift reached forward with his front leg and tripped the galloping brute.

Richey was taken completely by surprise.

He catapulted head over heels a few feet short of his target, smashing his head into the ground as he went.

Mo was finally back on his feet. He stared down at his confused opponent spread-eagled on the grass in the moonlight.

'What's the matter big boy?'

Drift backed away a fraction and stood perfectly still.

They both watched Richey stumble over and over and then back to his feet. Richey shook his head and stared at Mo and then the whippersnapper in turn.

'Where did he come from?' he whined. 'That was not fair!'

It didn't matter any longer what Richey said or thought. In the confusion he still hadn't realised the enormity of Drift's action. He couldn't see what all the others could see.

Both of Richey's antlers lay on the ground behind him.

'Oh!' said Richey, finally understanding his position. 'Oh no!'

As he was fond of doing, Mo winked at the beast.

'That is not fair! Not fair at all!' cried Richey.

'All's fair in love and war,' said Mo.

'But it simply was not fair! Two on to one is never fair!'

'Do you mean in antlers, or bodies?' asked Mo, winking at Drift this time.

'I could beat you anytime I wanted!' bragged Richey, glancing round at the hinds for support, but they had all turned their backs.

'So you want to fight on?' asked Mo, though he already knew the answer to that.

'No! Of course not! Not now! Not today! How could I? But next year, I will! Next year, you mark my words!'

'I will tell you what I will do, Richey. I will give you ten breaths to clear the field. After that…well…who can say…'

Richey looked longingly back at the herd who were now all gathered together down by the river, as if discussing the night's events, staring up at them, the moonlight picking out their eyes like diamonds.

'You haven't heard the last of me!' he yelled, his voice bouncing away across the valley before echoing back to them.

Heard the last of me!!! The last of me!!! Of Me!!! Of Me!!! Me!!! Me!!! Me!!! Me!!! Me!!!

'For this year, crocus face, I think we have,' said Mo.

Drift thought Richey was close to tears. It was a sad thing to see, a magnificent stag such as he reduced in that way, staring defeat in the eyes, but he had brought it on himself with his contemptuous attitude to all the other creatures in the forest. Drift had little pity for him, even when Richey finally skulked away.

Mo had won the day, in the end he had, and it was the right outcome. He had cleared the field of all his rivals, as was abundantly clear when the juvenile stags came forward to pay their respects, one by one, to affirm Mo's position as king of the herd. The old king had been defeated. Long live the new King!

'He will be back next year,' warned Drift. 'And he will be angrier and stronger than ever. We must prepare ourselves.'

'That's as may be,' said Mo, 'but a year is a long time in the life of the forest and things have a nasty habit of changing beyond the control of any creature.'

'You *are* the new King!' yelled Drift, glancing about at anyone who would dare dispute the fact.

No one did.

'Yes, I am,' said Mo calmly, reduced again to a single comical antler, his head already adopting the leaning look that had been there when Drift had first set eyes on him. 'I think it is time I introduced myself,' he said, though he didn't have to wander far, for all the hinds had now sauntered over to take a closer look at the new chief, the only red deer that was capable of putting the mean and ugly Big Richey to flight, well him, and the cute little one of course.

They would never forget the cute little one, there was something indefinably special about him, but for now the new chief was the stag known as uncle Mo, and that was the way it was meant to be, but everyone who had witnessed the day would go to sleep thinking of the cute little one known as Drift, the young one who had so bravely intervened and in the end, had decided the outcome, and the ultimate fate of the entire herd.

Eighteen

As it turned out Richey did not appear the following year and in truth no one really mourned his absence. A few months later a crazy mule named Swisher appeared on the fields. Swisher was so called because of his complete inability to keep his tail still for more than a second. Swisher occasionally performed manual labour for the humanthings down in the town in return for a big bag of carrots.

He told them an incredible thing. He had seen Big Richey in the town at the height of winter. It was a cold and frosty Saturday afternoon when Swisher witnessed Big Richey pulling a heavy sleigh, loaded with mini, squealing, humanthings. The sleigh was being driven by a weird man with a funny white beard dressed in a red tunic.

All the creatures thought that a ridiculously funny tale for Swisher was well known for his tall stories. The idea of Big Richey tethered to a sleigh was truly laughable and they giggled themselves silly at the thought of it, and afterwards, laughed the whole idea off as one of Swisher's silly pranks, despite the pendulum-tailed mule pleading otherwise. No one believed the crazy creature, except Drift.

He had seen the truth written in Swisher's eyes. He had heard the earnestness in the mad mule's voice. Swisher was telling the truth all right, and only Drift was perceptive enough to realise that. Drift kept his counsel and vowed that he would never sell his soul to the humanthings in that sad and sorry way. He would never allow himself to be bribed into labouring for those two-legged beings that brought so much sorrow to so many creatures. How could he, after what they had done to his own mother?

No one ever saw Big Richey again and in time he was soon forgotten, though the fight on the fields would be remembered for so long as deer roamed the forest. It is handed down, from one generation to the next, deerlore, valued and precious.

Bitter nights, short days, thunder and lightning, teeming rain, snowdrops, crocuses, catkins, daffodils, bluebells, tulips, long hot days, sultry nights, biting insects, golden trees, falling leaves, acorns and nuts, sharp frosts, thick snow, biting winds, bitter nights, short days, four happy years swirled by as the herd of red deer wandered the forest in search of the best feeding, and safety, and happiness.

Drift glanced up at the woodland. There was something vaguely familiar about this place. The tall trees were thinning as larger patches of good pasture took hold. Suddenly there was movement a little way ahead. Drift moved cautiously like a cat. He had become an expert in stealth. The very best, he could move anywhere in total silence. He was perfectly camouflaged as he peered through the trees toward the commotion ahead.

His sharp eyes focussed on the creature. It was a badger, an elderly badger with stiff joints and greying hair. Happy yelping floated through the air and from behind the old badger, one, two, three, four young ones boasting fresh black and white coats showed themselves, never once standing still, dashing hither and thither, and never straying far from the teacher.

Despite the arthritic movement there was something familiar about the old one. The same scruffy ears, the same short-sighted look on his face, as if permanently squinting through fog. Drift took three paces forward. It must be him. It had to be him.

'Daisy?' he asked calmly, in a deep voice that vibrated through the bushes and trees.

The badgers all took fright, the young ones rushing to shelter behind the big one. Strangers! Danger! You could not be too careful with strangers. Daisy slowly stood up to his full height and gazed at the fuzzy image standing between the two holly trees.

'Drift?' he said. 'Can that really be you?'

The stag nodded, his magnificent antlers swaying in the wind.

'Drift!' he shouted. 'Well just look at you! Look at you!'

The young ones were slowly growing bolder, dashing out for a quick inspection of the vast beast that now stood before them.

'I'd never have recognised you,' said Daisy.

'We all change in time, my friend.'

'That's a fact. You only have to look at me.'

'You don't look so bad.'

'It's good of you to say so.'

'And who are the little ones?'

'Come here and stand still for a moment,' ordered Daisy of the kits. 'This is someone I've always wanted you to meet. This is Drift, a red deer, one of the finest deer I have ever had the pleasure to meet.'

Drift nodded down at the kits, though he could tell they were still mighty wary of him, and rightly so.

Daisy spoke again. 'These are Joker, Tozer, Cheeky and Minx.'

'Pleased to meet you, Joker, Tozer, Cheeky and Minx,' said Drift.

'And us, you,' squealed Cheeky, who was clearly the boldest of the band. 'Is this the deer you told us you carried across the swollen river in days long ago, uncle Daisy?'

Drift smirked at Daisy.

'I didn't say that exactly, it wasn't quite like that,' muttered Daisy uncomfortably.

'And they are yours?' asked Drift.

'Good heavens, no. They are all orphans, their mother, you know, came to grief, on the highway.'

'Ah,' said Drift. 'I can sympathise with that.'

'Well of course you can,' said Daisy. 'I was forgetting myself. I am slowly teaching them things, you understand, though it is taking longer than I thought. I am their guardian.'

'Such as where they are most likely to find a hamburger, no doubt,' teased Drift.

Daisy smiled. 'Well yes, that, and many other things too.'

'Then they are the most lucky of creatures,' said Drift. 'They couldn't possibly have a better teacher.'

'You are kind to say so, Drift. But you were always most kind.'

Drift sniffed the air and waggled his head.

'There is someone I'd like you to meet.'

'Oh yes, and who might that be?'

The stag glanced back over his right shoulder.

'Come and join us!'

Once again the kits ran for cover as a striking hind dashed from the trees and ran up and stood beside Drift and smiled down at the badgers. Daisy peered up through his rheumy eyes in admiration for this was something special. Light brown sparkling eyes framed in long lashes; and a long slender neck on the most beautiful red deer hind he had ever seen.

'This is Snowflake,' said Drift, unable to keep the pride from his voice. 'We are going to have fawns all of our own.'

Snowflake flushed. 'That is not for you to decide, Drift de Mottisfont. Only the Great Stag in the sky can decide such matters.'

'That's as may be,' muttered Drift, 'but you knows what I intends.'

'De Mottisfont?' queried Daisy, a smirk plastered across his grey face.

'An old family name apparently,' explained Drift. 'I didn't even know we had such a thing until uncle Mo told me all about it. I don't bother with it myself you understand, but you know what hinds can be like.'

Daisy nodded. 'Quite so, I suppose I do. How is your uncle Mo by the way?'

'He is well enough, though not the creature he was. I am the King Stag now. It took a little getting used to for the old man at first, but now he lives with us happily. He says it was my destiny.'

'I always knew you would rise to such a lofty position. There was something special about you, young Drift, an inner desire to achieve things, a steeliness that I have seen only in a very few creatures of the forest.'

Drift was happy to hear such things.

'Will you be staying around these parts for long?' asked Daisy

'Only today. I have promised to take Snowflake down to Blue China Farm to where the humanthing can actually speak.'

'I don't believe a word of it,' teased Snowflake. 'I have never heard such a ridiculous thing, and I will never believe it until I hear it with my own ears.'

''Tis true,' said Daisy, 'as true as I am standing here. The humanthing can speak to the creatures.'

'We shall see all about that,' said Snowflake, glancing at Drift and back at the badger, 'won't we Drift?'

'We shall see so long as we can find the strange one known as Helena.'

'She'll be much older now,' said Daisy.

'That applies to us all,' said Drift.

Daisy nodded his head once more and then said: 'Will you be returning to these parts again?' a note of hopefulness hidden in his cracking voice.

'Yes, most certainly, but not for another season.'

'Methinks I shall be away by then,' said Daisy, glancing down at the ever-active young ones, and back at Drift. 'If you understand my meaning. Just so long as I can leave these bundles of fun in a better way than I found them.'

'I understand completely,' said Drift. 'I never had the chance to thank you properly for all you did for me.'

'Yes you did!' grinned Daisy. 'Ten times over, so far as I recall!'

'Perhaps I did at that. I can't quite remember.'

'Come on then,' said Snowflake, eager to be away, becoming impatient as hinds sometimes do. 'Are you going to show me this strange farm housing even stranger creatures or not?'

Drift and Daisy shared another look.

Drift rolled his eyes.

Daisy smirked, and somehow deep in the depths of that smirk lay hidden and happy memories from long ago.

'Goodbye old fella,' said Drift. 'Make sure you enjoy every day the sun comes up.'

'And you the same, and look after that fine hind of yours, or someone else will.'

'You can rely on that,' said Drift, turning about, and then back for a second. 'But we had some fun though, didn't we?'

'Aye. We surely did,' agreed Daisy. 'I think the very best of days. I wouldn't have missed them for the world.'

Drift bowed his head to the five badgers that were by then all lined up in front of him. They stared up in awe at the majesty of the beast, the power that was so clearly within him, but also at the gentleness and dignity he displayed. This stag clearly was the king of the forest, no one could ever deny that, a wise and handsome beast, and more than that, he was a close and personal friend of their very own uncle Daisy.

'Goodbye!' shrieked the kits in unison. 'You will come and see us again, won't you?'

'We will,' said Drift and Snowflake as one. 'For sure. We will. We'll bring the whole family next time,' said Drift.

Drift and Daisy exchanged one final look, and in the next moment the pair of deer were cantering happily away beneath the trees, chattering as they went, searching for the track that would eventually lead down to that strange place known as Blue China Farm.

The forest in autumn is one of God's great sights when the leaves turn colour and bask in that special golden light. The forest is home to many magical creatures and toward the end of the year it provides the greatest spectacle on earth. Nothing compares, nor ever will. Love the forest, while you can.

- If you enjoyed this book you might like to note that a new expanded, illustrated edition is planned for next year, plus an audio CD version. You can read updates of that and much more besides and lodge feedback and reviews on the website www.driftandbadger.com

Drift and Badger and the Search for Uncle Mo

Also Available from TrackerDog Media:

The Fish Catcher

Mary and Daisy Fissleborough are sisters evacuated from the East End of London in the early part of World War II. They are taken 200 miles to the west and dumped on people they have never met before. It isn't long before Mary is looking at the affairs of Wolfdale Hall through a quizzical eye. Where is the daughter Cicely? Why is her room always locked? And who is the strange man Oliver Tresco who lolls about the place doing nothing? Why is he not in the armed forces too?

Find out more about the sisters
and read the entire first chapter right now at:

www.thefishcatcher.co.uk

"A well-written mystery with a fascinating touch of historical fact. A novel suitable for both older children and adults, which I would **Highly Recommend** to both generations."
Reviewer: Cheryl Ellis, Allbooks Review
Available through all good bookstores quoting ISBN: 978-1-84753-930-4

**Interested in Renting Property?
Interested in Starting Your Own Property Business From Home?
Do You Have Property To Let?**

If so, you need:

SPLAM!

**Successful Property Letting
And Management
ISBN: 9780955977404**

**New revised and expanded edition OUT NOW.
SPLAM! is available from all good bookstores.**

**Take a look at
www.splam.co.uk**
*for more information.
Available in download or hardcopy format*

Drift and Badger and the Search for Uncle Mo

<u>Coming Soon From TrackerDog Media</u>

Grist Vergette's Curious Clock

Grist Vergette passed away on the 200th anniversary of the Battle of Trafalgar. In his will he leaves his grandson Johnny the key to his garden shed. But why? Johnny meets Seri, the daughter of their German neighbours, and hurries down to the allotments where the shed lies abandoned in the far corner beneath the laburnum tree.

The large key opens the shed and ultimately a doorway to untold treasures. But this is a garden shed whose primary purpose is most certainly not for gardening.

They find a box crammed with strange artefacts from long ago, including a most peculiar clock bearing only ten numbers. Johnny fiddles with the clock but it does not work. It is broken, useless, and he tosses it to one side. But minutes later the alarm on the clock goes off and sets in place a sequence of events that will change the lives of Johnny and Seri forever. You can follow them too, but only in Grist Vergette's Curious Clock.

Grist's Vergette's Curious Clock is coming soon from TrackerDog Media. For more information and a release date please email TrackerDog Media at:

<u>supalife@aol.com</u>

Over 1,000,000 CLASSIFIED ADS, Broken Down by Country, City, and Categories In An EASY-TO-USE Site.

Homemax Adpost is one of the most popular online classifieds sites. It attracts more than 10,000,000 views every month and generates more than 10,000 ads and replies every day across its network.

To check out the site that offers FREE basic services for VIRTUALLY EVERYTHING YOU NEED IN CLASSIFIEDS, please visit:

http://homemax.adpost.com/

This site is a great resource!

www.ingramcontent.com/pod-product-compliance
Ingram Content Group UK Ltd.
Pitfield, Milton Keynes, MK11 3LW, UK
UKHW041436180426
11947UKWH00007B/477